SKY ROBERT

A FATED MATES ALIEN ROMANCE

Broken Books

Redmond, WA 98052

First published in the United States of America by Broken Books LLC, 2025

Copyright © 2025 S.M. McCoy, Sky Robert

ISBN: 978-1-963669-01-5

Cover Art by Deborah Garcia

Editing by Amaze Inn Proofreading

All Rights Reserved

To you, the readers, that have supported my author journey. This story wouldn't exist without your excitement for the Trillume Universe!

TABLE OF CONTENTS

Trillume Glossary

Trillume Universe...

All books in the Trillume Universe are standalone. There is no need to have read any other book before this one, in fact, this standalone takes place before all other events written about in the rest of the series!

The Trillume Universe is currently under attack by a species called the Solusgor, and in an effort to save many planets from being destroyed by this virus of a species, the trill have developed nanotechnology to stop its replication. They are uncertain of the lasting, long-term effects of this "cure", and with lives on the line... they don't care. A group of warriors from the Galactic Authority are tasked with distributing the nanobots to the far reaches of the galaxy in hopes of cutting the species off before they can reach more concentrated civilizations and mass casualties.

GLOSSARY

Alien Stats:

Estrelds: a community-driven clan on the planet Estreldez that are dependent on radiation from their moons that are absorbed through the many jewels on their skin. Their planet is rather isolated, but for a mating ceremony that they have opened to offworld participation due to the fertility crisis. Their skin coloring has been known to be in many shades of blue, green, purple, and pink. The brightness of their skin, and the quantity of their jewels, called loh, are indicators of strong virility and highly sought after in mates. Find out more about Estrelds in Jewel of the Alien Bandit.

Krelins: a hive-mind warrior species on the planet Krelis that can communicate with their hive through great distances through their horns and allows for unparalleled coordination with their warfleets. They are ruled by a single queen and are usually aggressive by nature, with a history of taking things by force. They have wings, stingers in their forearms, and horns that transmit communication to the hive. Find out more about the Krelins in Her Alien Prince.

Trills: a poisonous, reptilian species that comes in shades of green (probably where the rumors of little green men from human lore come from) but they are anything but little, and they are an intelligent, strategic conqueror of the known universe who have come into power with alliances across worlds that no one has yet to defy with the necia warriors as their enforcers.

Necias: a warrior species that are known as the enforcers of the Trillume Universe under the direct command of the trill. They have a secondary exoskeleton that comes out like sharp spikes from their shoulders, arms, legs, and back. They are like a walking weapon. (More details about these species are included in Her Alien Savior and Her Alien Warrior)

Humans: Within this universe they are part of an exchange program being sent out on cultural exchanges with other planets in exchange for goods and sciences.

UnGors: discussed briefly as a warrior and tribe like species with tentacles hidden within their hair. They commonly braid in bones with their coming-of-age ceremonies as they grow, and you can tell an unGor's age based on how long their "hair" is, as the hair is not hair at all.

Shol: a rare species that has all but been annihilated from the Solusgors attack on their planet. They have fangs, and runes on their body. They mate once in their life and have known to go insane if their mate dies before they do. More details about shol in Jewel of the Alien Bandit.

There are more species in the universe including the briefly talked about species the Sumtra: A fish-like species that has bright blue hair when out of the water, and light green skin, but when they are submerged in water, their bodies become reflective, and their hair turns the same color as the kelp to better camouflage with the elements. More to come from this species in an upcoming book.

Bina: farthest moon

Dendil: the tongue/language of Estreldez

Emon: the mother/foster caretaker of the offspring training facility on Estreld

Galactic Trill Authority: the enforcers of the universe

Ganpan-fal: world destroyer

Glilor reptiles near the waterholes they blink with a second eyelids

Glorbin Flower: Ordin Crystal on Estreldez, a highly condensed fuel source for space travel

Goddess Lumei: Trill goddess

Goddess of Lenkal: Krelis goddess

Hergslat : an animal that resembles a large rodent with many clawed legs, and tusks, used to help quarry the stones and jewels because their anger made them perfect for smashing the rocks into manageable chunks, and we never had to mistreat the beasts because they were easy to migrate, and raging helped them file down their claws.

Hewve lard: Prime import from Krelis to Estreldez (food import)

Human Exchange Trade—H.E.T.—

Kan: the horns of a krelin on their head in their tongue it means to feel or sense

Ki: the horns that come from a krelin's wrists/stingers

Loh: jewels that absorb the radiation of the moons on estrelds

Lupa: largest moon of the planet called Estreldez

Molt fever: krelin sickness

M.R. Team: Moon Mating Research

Ordin Crystal: Glorbin Flower on Estreldez

Pan: moon stone, also means heart in Dendil (language of Estreldez)

Romta shells: hard minerals found by the water on Estreldez. Discarded shells created from a Romta creature's spit and rock dust. Often used as a first food after an estreld's teeth come in as an offspring, many offspring spit on them to help soften them more for eating.

Root of arnut: Poisonous vein within the deep parts of mountain rock, can be ground up and ingested to cause forced abortion of early pregnancy.

Sulltid: a curse word on Trillume, a parasite that if not detected in time cause brain bleeds and result similar to stroke victims or death.

Strel: language of the estrelds (renamed by hoomans) to all Estreldez the language is Dendil.

Tarnpul: black rock on Estreldez that is used to absorb the moon's radiation and magnify it.

Queen Kai: Krelis Queen

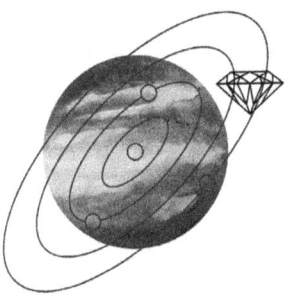

Chapter One

Hazel

B lue blood dried within my fingernails from digging at the mountain rocks for food. I spat on them so they could soak into the pores, softening them for eating, but my mouth was so dry that it did little to help. I would have to return to the fresh-water deposit close to the clan. There was no reason for anyone to visit the waterfall, considering they had underground pipes that brought the drinking water to the center of the city, but it was pretty at night.

Couples would sneak out of the clan to pleasure themselves there in secret. Though, I wasn't sure it was all that much of a secret, since they didn't care if other couples were there or not. I wasn't supposed to get that close to see anything. The water was easily accessed from the river at the top of the waterfall, where I would come down from the mountain. Going that close to the waterfall was mostly because the water was cleaner there. At least, that's what I told myself.

With an empty nectar pot, wrapped up in strong rope that I could use to carry it on my back, I set off to the waterfall that my mother had told me never to get too close to when she was alive. I'd disobeyed her many times to watch the other estrelds together. I wasn't a spawnling anymore, and I liked hearing the noises they made. With her return to the great rock, she was no longer around to warn me, or to keep me company. It was tiring to live on my own, abandoned in a mountain cave, and outcast from the clan.

Perhaps, that was why I went to the waterfall. One rising, I would be spotted by someone, and they would take me back to the Almder and back to the clan. I'd seen her at one of the mating ceremonies that my mom snuck off to. I caught her and she told me that this was the only time I could visit the clan when I was old enough. When everyone was too distracted with mating, and no one cared who you were. That was a long time ago, and I'd been too scared to get that close to the clan on my own.

My mother was cast out, and if she returned, she'd be executed. With her gone, would they accept me?

I heard the moans of a female in pleasure over the sound of water splashing from the small cliff drop into the pool, and I smiled wryly as I quickly unstrapped my nectar pot. In my hurry, the pot wobbled as I put it down and I had to return to right it before it toppled. At the top of the falls, there was a smooth rock I would sit on that overlooked the pool below where the noises were coming from. My loh jewels along my light-green skin glowed the closer I got, and then I saw her within the dusky glow of the water. It was late, but many plants and rocks on this side of the mountain were infused with the moon's radiation giving everything a beautiful luminance at night.

She was by herself, and in her hands was a finely shaped rock of black tarnpul like a tube jutting from the rock that she rubbed her mating loh against between her thighs. Her loh jewels glowed across her bright blue skin as her hips bucked in the air, up and down the shaft attached to the rock until I saw her mating loh activate, creating an opening. She laughed with excitement before she adjusted herself to her knees and wrapped a hand around the rock, sinking her mating loh on top until the rock disappeared inside her little by little. Her deep moan of satisfaction ignited something inside of me that made my own hips jolt for friction.

My breathing quickened as the rock I sat on rubbed against the loh between my legs. I watched as the female lifted herself up and worked the shaft in and out, her panting growing louder as I bit my lip to stop myself from voicing the cry that worked its way up my throat as my own mating loh glowed, begging to be filled, but with nothing around but a smooth rock to move against. As she shuddered against the rock, so did I, finding a kind of pleasure greater than simply watching others seek out their own pleasure, but mine as well.

Between my thighs a throbbing grew, making my hand claps over myself to stop the empty feeling, only to find my mating loh had split, allowing my fingertips to sink in. I gasped and pushed my slender, but rough fingers deeper, only to hiss at the tenderness of my nailbeds from digging up rocks earlier.

"Sodenmare," I cursed at the moons. It had felt so good before that, and I wanted more, but it wouldn't be my fingers filling me today, not with how sore they were.

"Don't stop on my account," a glib deep voice I didn't recognize startled me from beyond the bushes that grew along the river. I froze in place, and the bushes rustled with movement. They were one of the few plants that didn't have a glow to them and there was nothing but shadows within them. One particularly large one emerged, but I recognized the shape of wings and horns.

Krelin!

Stumbling back off the rock, I tried to disappear within the bushes behind me to avoid confronting him. It wouldn't be difficult for me to stay hidden and make my way back to the cave. I knew this mountain better than anyone.

Then a hand wrapped around my mouth before I could scream. "Shhh, we can't have you alerting the pretty blue one down below," another krelin that had been behind me warned.

I thrashed against his hold, but a dizzy feeling made me too weak, and my muscles felt as wild as the water close by. The smell of something sweet, sweeter than anything I'd ever experienced burned down my nose and touched the back of my tongue. My loh flickered out, the glow gone from the pleasure I once felt, and the krelin chuckled in my ear. The shadow in front of me floated off the ground, a buzzing sound filled the air, mixed with the rolling waters of the falls it could almost be considered calming. If it weren't for the terror that consumed me as I watched the dark figure of the krelin fly down to where the other female was, basking in the moon's rays... with her eyes closed.

No! I screamed in my head.

Krelins were terrifying with their large horns, sharp claws, long fangs, and wings that made them quick to escape. But what was more terrifying was what he said next, "You know, taking you doesn't violate any laws from my planet or yours. You should have stayed safe in your clan's territory, because our trade treaty doesn't protect you out here. Estrelds aren't considered a tradeable good on your planet, so it isn't considered stealing anything, and I'm not harming you either. I can't say the same for your wellbeing after you're sold, but every krelin is bound by the Queen's will."

He spoke as if it wasn't the first time he'd relayed the information to pre-emptively stop any protest I might have to him swooping his arm under my knees until he was carrying my limp body. Struggling to keep the numbness from taking over my mind, I tried to stay awake. The laws of Estreldez weren't something I knew much about, living outside the clan my whole life, but now I was upset with my mom more than I had ever been before. It wasn't right to curse the dead, but it was whatever sin she committed that had us outcast, and because of that, I might never see the inside of the clan or seek out its protections ever again.

"And the Queen's will is that this planet is ours."

Chapter Two

Yueril of the Trillume Authority

P ulling into the desolate space junk that was nothing more than a dead rock, void of anything but imported trades to its name, would be the only celebration my crew would have for a while. We were to set off farther into the robe's edge of the sector, that was not yet ravaged by the Solusgors, once the first cargo was dropped on Delta Fal. The chill of space made my scales flare up the sides of my head. I didn't have to say a word to my second in command, Belder, for her to know what was circling my thoughts. It was on all of our minds.

"Will recruiting these volatile species to our ranks deter the Solusgors from invading?" Belder asked. She was as skeptical as I was about the success reported from our queen on Necias Prime.

My jaw tightened with guilt. Even our queen knew it would not be enough. Our princess, Klemon, said as much before I departed on my mission. The queen would attempt to bring in a warrior species that could act as an "appearance" of strength to ease the planets under our protection from worry. History would not look kindly on my involvement in what would be needed to be done to protect this galaxy. The cost would be high. Should someone try to undo our efforts... death would come swiftly.

Could I live with myself for what I have done? What I was doing by releasing our cargo on this planet?

I would have to. At least we would all live.

Have mercy on the few for what must be done for the many.

I took a steady breath to answer her. "It isn't about whether or not they join us," I admitted.

"You think so? The threat that they might be strong enough to defeat the Solusgors could be enough, could it not?"

Involuntarily, I couldn't help my head shaking in the negative, revealing a truth I didn't want to burden her with.

"It will have to be. For now, we will celebrate the news that our queen succeeded, while we were away, to recruit a fierce warrior planet to protect this universe and all the planets within it."

The necia warriors were living weapons, and somehow our queen was able to use their own laws to convince them to join us. But having a show of force wouldn't be enough to stop the Solusgors. It was a show of false security. Only recently was I given access to the records of what the threat truly was. They didn't care about who was out here, how strong they were, or who they killed. And their technology was world destroying.

"I'm not sure how much celebrating we'll be doing on an outlaw planet that doesn't have any loyalties to Trillume..."

She had a point. I would hardly call Delta Fal a planet, and the outlaws here required us to stay alert.

"This is our last stop before we return to Trillume, unless our orders change. It will still take many rotations before we see home again. Enjoy the change of scenery while you can, Belder."

"It is what is not seen that we must embrace in multitudes," she agreed with a bow of her head, seeking my forgiveness for not seeing the gift of having this small luxury before a long journey home. We had little in the way of supplies, and what we gathered on this outlaw planet would be what we had to return with.

If we returned at all, I did not dare say it out loud. The queen knew what she was asking of my crew and myself when she sent us. Our technology was great, but traveling this distance was still a gamble. If there weren't enough supplies on this barren rock, there would be no return for us. No future once our activities were discovered.

"Enjoy the time we have," I reiterated for both of our sakes. Belder swallowed deeply, the scales on her neck flexed with discomfort. Her green skin darkened at the small slice visible from the top of her robes, where she had undoubtedly pulled at her neckline in search of relief that wouldn't come from shedding the weight of our clothes.

I adjusted my own robes tighter around myself and grunted as the confirmation of our ship docking at the planet's orbit station appeared on the display panel.

It was time...

I flipped the switch for cargo bays seven and eight, releasing the bioweapon on an already barren planet filled with outlaws and unfortunate souls that were but a casualty of protecting the universe from the Solusgors.

They would live: the scientists assured me that its purpose was to stop the replication of the virus.

The Solusgors weren't a species as we pictured it, though that was what had been said about them. Giving them a form gave our warriors and our clan something to stand against. A "them" to stand before and unite against.

The warriors from Necias Prime were but a facade to make the planets under our care feel safe.

They would be safer, I thought, with zero amusement at what this would cost us all.

"Is it done?" Belder tore me from my dark thoughts.

I nodded, and my crew prepared to launch the shuttle towards the surface. Cargo bay seven was connected with our shuttle transports. Cargo bay eight connected with the docking station orbiting the planet... Every ship would carry the nanobots with them. From bandits across the stars, it will spread to planets we couldn't reach on our own.

This would be the origin of what would be the most devastating attack on the entire universe, and I was its harbinger.

Belder didn't know the full extent of our mission. She knew enough to know that what I just unleashed on this planet and on our crew might mean we never made it home again.

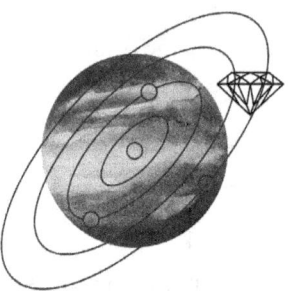

Chapter Three
Hazel

The radiation pack I huddled next to for warmth was growing colder by the rotation. It cost my dignity to get it, but it was better than where I was headed to. If that unGor spawn on the slave ship hadn't looked the other way when loading the rest of the marked ones... I wouldn't have a life to complain about. The Zorn would surely punish him if he found out he had been soft in his duties. Genbi. I'll never forget the name or his kindness.

"Find a way back to your planet," he told me before he shuddered. He grimaced down his nose—like what he saw in my future were the nightmares of things I would not wish on my enemies, let alone someone as young as him. He barely reached the height of my shoulders, and though I was tall for many species, I knew from seeing others of his kind on the trader's ship that his species grew quite large. It was common for estreld females like myself to be of similar height to the males. I was no different in that regard.

Genbi's hair was short and braided at the top, with only two bones for adornment. If his height hadn't told me of his age, the length of his hair and minimal bones would have confirmed it. When I later asked about unGors from other outlaws, before they saw my mark, they said an unGor's hair was a roadmap of their life. Genbi's was only beginning. I hoped he too would find a way to escape being under the Zorn's rule. He was the largest outlaw in this sector, and many of the pirates here avoided me I asked about him. Word spread of my mark. Even the hint that I might have escaped from the Zorn's trading route made many of them fearful. If they were seen with me, rumors were that the Lord Zorn would think that they stole me themselves. None of them even wanted to return me to him because they didn't want the Lord Zorn to mistake their involvement, or even be associated with an unclaimed slave.

It was both a blessing and a curse. The outlaws left me alone, but I struggled to find a way back to my home planet, Estreldez, and I was running out of hope.

My bones cracked as I forced myself to seek out food. Turning off my radiation pack, that I buried under the crusty dirt of a dark alley, I weakly made my way to the heap of trash near the landing strip, where shuttles didn't care about keeping the streets clean. The clucking sound of krelins had me cowering behind a dirty moat of water that was likely toxic to consume, not that I had much choice when this planet didn't have any rivers or much life besides a quick detour for outlaws to hideout or trade goods.

There were regular ships that all they did was transport supplies the outlaws would need to restock their ships with. But many species didn't have the same kind of digestion that I did, and as soon as I heard the krelins disembark from their shuttle, I cried.

Part fear and part relief flooded through me. Krelins were the reason I was here, but the last time they visited was the reason I was still alive. They tossed a bucket of rocks on the ground, and a strange animal slithered behind them. It had no legs, and yet it moved. It had fins below its mouth but had no eyes and it made the most calming sound, like a whistle of wind through a glade as the moon's glow warmed your skin.

For a brief moment, the creature's sound distracted me from the departing krelins. Their wings buzzed in unison with the whistle, before I remembered to mold myself against the trash heap so their horns couldn't sense I was here.

The krelins could talk to each other through the hive bond, and their horns could track things around them without use of their sight. I never knew why they took me, but they were the closest planet to Estreldez, and if I could find a way to stay hidden on their ship... a sliver of hope returned for the chance that I could return home, and I dove for the rocks scattered on the dry dirt, spitting on them to soften the chunks before biting down.

I didn't care what the rocks were. The krelins tossed them like they were garbage, but to me they were food. The flavor was sweet, and unlike the rocks on Estreldez, they crumbled under the pressure of my teeth with little effort, melting in my mouth like a treat. Spitting on them was simply habit from eating shiny romta shells as an offspring. I could even break these rocks apart with my fist, and eat it with nibbles that filled my stomach, and warmed my loh.

"Excuse me," a friendly male voice intruded on my meal. No one dared speak with me, I thought. His voice was startling because I didn't know if I was imagining it, but also that he had snuck up so close without me noticing.

I glanced up from gathering the rocks and saw he held one out for me that had rolled from the pile out of my hurried clumsiness. He held the rock curiously, and I narrowed my eyes at him with suspicion.

His wrinkled nose could be seen from the shadows of his robes before he ripped off a piece of his robe with a deft tug of strength. He wrapped the rock in it and then offered it again. I'd never seen his species before and I couldn't take my eyes off of him. He had three fingers that were quite large, and I could see the tip of his claws peeking through his vibrant green skin that he had retracted to show he was not a threat. I knew better than to trust such things, but the warmth of knowing I would eat today had addled my mind.

Such vibrancy of color was a sign of health and strength for an estreld male, and I was always so jealous that I was born female with such a muted, pale color that only worsened with the lack of my moon's radiation to absorb into my loh. But this male, he was stunning in all the shades of green that seemed to reflect and glow in the dingy light of the shuttle landing strip. It was almost iridescent how his scales shifted and sparkled, as if he was covered in stars. And I was only admiring his face and outreached hand. He wore a flowing black robe, embroidered in a similar shade of yellow like the creases of his scales. A few flared along his temples, pushing back his hood just a bit more before he pulled it forward with his other hand, hiding much of him in shadow.

A tingling sensation ran up my back and into my shoulder blades as I watched him. I reached up to my hair, self-conscious-ly aware that I was dirty, and I'd been forced to cut my hair as part of the price for my radiation core. I stupidly entertained the idea of his opinion of me to prevent myself from acknowl-edging that I was nothing more than a fugitive slave, or that he was anything other than a lawbreaker who came to this lifeless planet to commit unspeakable deeds. I snatched the wrapped rock from his hand.

He didn't sneer or back away. With a simple smile that kept his teeth hidden, another sign of trying to pretend he was no threat, he then said, "I have scanned the contents of your meal, and have determined that it is actually highly nutritious, but is not compatible with my own tastes." He couldn't hide the sharp rows of points behind his lips as he spoke. Those teeth were not suitable for that kind of diet, but for meals that were once living. He was a predatory species, and I was prey.

I wouldn't tell him, but I was relieved to know that the food was not dangerous. Even if I didn't have much of a choice if it were.

"Forgive me if this is presumptuous," he continued. "But would you be willing to escort me to where someone would rest on this planet?"

He didn't use the name of the planet, and either he was a very good actor, or he was a rare visitor and would be picked dry before he ever stepped foot on his shuttle again, if he ever did.

To confirm my suspicions, I didn't meet his eyes again while I unwrapped the strip of his robe and repacked it with more mystery rocks, for easier carrying. "You'll find the Den of Bounty after the junk trader's tent. You can't miss it." I pointed the wrong way, though what I said was true, and he simply nodded and stood from his crouch.

His eyes were a dark brown, almost the color of tarnpul, and just as absorbing. It was like staring at them could drain me of whatever radiation I held on to, and I couldn't deny them their claim. Happily, I would fall through those depths. They didn't give me that accustomed look of disgust, or the lingering fear of who I was associated with.

"In many we rise," he said with a bow of his head, like I was more than the dirt beneath his boots. He didn't speak in my native tongue, but whatever implant the Lord Zorn gave me included languages of every species that had passed through this outpost.

His platitude sounded as if he were speaking directly to the soul of many species not born as meat-eating predators. As part of a clan, we were strong, and by ourselves, we were prey.

I groaned at the way his words made me think that perhaps he was different from the other outlaws. He was kind, and I would return the favor this once by giving him proper direction. "The den is the other way."

He simply nodded and adjusted his strides without questioning why I had lied to him to begin with.

Curiosity got the better of me as I followed him from a distance. Not once did he turn to show he noticed he had an extra set of eyes on him. My fingers brushed through my short, tangled green hair. It wasn't a pretty green like his skin, just a dull pale green like the dirt from the glorbin flower mines. My mother used to say that my coloring was special because, just like tarnpul, everyone would wish to keep me close to protect them one day.

I scoffed at the memory. I was young, foolish even, to believe her. It was because of her foolishness of wishing to keep me to herself, and not giving me to the offspring breeding facilities, that I was alone when she passed... Alone when the krelins took me.

I may never forgive her, I thought with a deep ache in my loh that vibrated deep within my ribcage.

The handsome stranger made it to the den, and I huddled against the tent of the junk dealer. The unsettling owner of the tent whispered beside me in her strange lilt, "What is someone else's waste, is another's treasure."

"You know I have nothing to trade." I flinched and backed away as I felt my loh throb with warning at her closeness. They remembered what I had traded the last time I was here.

Her long finger traced along my arm and over my loh as she muttered, "You've got jewels on your skin. Fine enough trade for me. Your last one fetched a pretty price from an unGor a red star ago."

"They aren't stones, they are my skin," I sneered with disgust at what I was forced to give just to stay alive.

"Skin, stone," the creepy dealer dismissed with a shrug of her shoulder. "I've sold plenty of furs and scales over the years. Those are someone's skin too, yes?"

"I'm not giving you my loh," I had to repeat, but I doubted the woman with the gray skin and oddly vibrant blue eyes cared what I said. She knew better than most that desperation came for all of us on this planet.

"Haven't seen his kind on Delta Fal since this desolate rock was simply a place they dumped survivors of the Shol Star War."

"A war?" It was hard not to listen to anything the old crone had to say. She was the only one who'd speak with me, and I didn't even care what she talked about, only that she spoke with me.

"Oh yes, I was too young to remember the war, but I've been on Delta Fal before there was a docking station or a pirate lord's claim. Delta Fal is a common phrase on Sholonus, meaning Fated Death."

That was disheartening to hear, but when I took my eyes off the entrance to the den to stare at her, she was smiling with sharp fangs drawn. The old survivor cackled before she shook her head with amusement.

"Outlaws think this a fitting name for their outpost, but between you and me, to a shol, it is a promise of retribution. A second rising, if you will. It was not a hopeless name, but one of power and a dream of a future."

"Why are you telling me this?"

The crooked dealer hadn't spoken much to me, even if she was the only one who was willing to say anything at all.

"If the trill have returned, then something has shifted in the universe, and you must find out what."

"Excuse me?"

She had lost her mind.

"You want off this rock, and I can arrange that for a price. I told you a bit of my story because freedom is often not enough to motivate someone to do what must be done. I don't care that you escaped Lord Zorn or not. The trill are a wise species, and though they are deadly, they do not often fight. He is not the only trill on this planet. A whole crew of them have arrived and, according to the ones that raised me, they came when the sickness was spreading through Sholonus.

"Instead of helping my species, they destroyed our planet to prevent the spread of the Star Sickness. Shol survivors were only left alone after extensive tests and even then, we were left to die on a barren planet with little resources."

I was covering my mouth as if that would put the unspeakable back within her throat from which they were spoken. Her whole planet was destroyed and, if she was to be believed, then the trill were only here for one reason, to give renewed meaning to the planet's name, Delta Fal, Fated Death.

Chapter Four
Yueril

The den was cleaner than I had expected, and when I asked for a room, they led me to a viewing screen filled with monitors of every available accommodation, both to show that I would be watched, and to see each pod offering would include its own companion for my stay. Off to the other wall was a rotation of security cameras, one of which was constantly on the exits. My eye caught on the discarded emerald of the streets as she clutched the flaps of the junk trader's tent outside.

The edge of my lips quirked up in delight that I had been correct about her following me. From the moment I saw her huddled amongst the debris of the shuttle strip, my vision narrowed, and it took everything within my willpower to stop myself from summoning my team to raze the city. I could, with a simple command, overrun this entire port with my crew, but I had instructed them to take rotations of only a shuttle's amount at a time for their celebrations of what they believed was a victory of the planet Necias Prime joining the galactic authority.

Only Belder knew our mission was more than posting up at an outlaw base to stand off against the threat of the Solusgor's approach. Every warrior under my command was prepared to die to protect the universe, but there was no preparation for what we would face when they arrived. They weren't an entity of flesh and blood.

"Who is that?" I asked of my escort.

He cleared his throat and tried to motion me back to the other viewing screens. "No one wants to be caught with a branded slave of Lord Zorn without proof that you've paid your dues. That one can't be touched until Lord Zorn returns, but I do have plenty of other options for every taste of the universe for your stay."

I clenched my jaw to control myself and kept my voice even as I demanded, "Bring her to my room." A slave! My scales threatened to spray the whole room with a toxin to subdue them all.

The spindly-looking escort chewed on his lip nervously, unsure of what to make of me, or what kind of outlaw I must be. "I mean no disrespect, but if you do not know who Lord Zorn is... it's best not to be anywhere near that one. As pretty as she is, she isn't worth your life, as that is what it will cost you."

"I'll decide what it will cost me," I hissed and as his throat bobbed, he then nodded his understanding.

"I'll have her delivered tonight, but I will warn you, the last outlaw to touch the property of Lord Zorn met an untimely end. It won't matter if you plan on paying him after, that you were just looking out for her, or if you claim to inform him that you found her and wanted to return her... Be prepared to defend your life. He'd rather everyone know that escaping isn't an option for a slave, that no one will help them, because if they do, everyone who has been in contact with them will die. Her best option is to wait for Lord Zorn and return to him for her punishment."

My scales flared along my skull, forcing my hood back as I sneered, displaying my sharp teeth. He flinched, and I reiterated that I wouldn't be intimidated by a male that ruled with fear. "When you bring her to my room, you will tell her that it is a request that the Emerald Treasure show a presumptuous wanderer around for his stay. In exchange, the room is hers for as long as she'd like." I watched him carefully to reiterate, "A request. I will know if you have forced her to join me, and it will be you who pays the price."

He sputtered, "I cannot keep her at the den, word will spread, and I will—"

24

I cut him off. "You are not the owner of this establishment." It was clear from his fear that he was nothing more than a caretaker in the real owner's absence.

Behind us, a clucking noise had both our attentions turning to the viewing room entrance, where a warrior spread out his leathery wings in intimidation. My escort cowered, making himself seem small with his shoulders hunched. This may be someone with a bit more authority here.

He looked over at the screen, where my treasure used to be. She was gone, no longer peeking from behind the dealer's tent. Then the newcomer dipped his horns to me with a smile. "Forgive my associate. He forgets that the customer is always right. If there is someone you want us to bring to you, we will. You do understand that you will take full responsibility for whatever repercussions come from our procurement, so we'll require the fee upfront."

"Commander..." the meek one warned against the offer.

A stern stare was all he got in return, but he nodded profusely. The clucking sound from deep in his throat was forming a pattern that sounded more and more like a language not covered by our databases.

"You will follow Commander Goen," my escort suggested while backing away.

Replacing my hood over my head, I followed without hesitation. I was alone, but I was not unarmed, despite being searched when I entered.

He spoke as we walked through the well-kept halls, a vast contradiction to the exterior of the den. "I've acquired a species that struggles to thrive on my planet, but my queen believes the flightless worms make a welcome change to the taste of our nectar. I've been tasked with bringing more, since the first gave us a strong kantos spawn. She believes we need another worm to help her hatch the new generation. That is where you come in. It is the price for my establishment risking the wrath of Lord Zorn. You are to make sure this worm will survive longer than the last."

"And you believe I can do that for you?" I asked, incredulous at the assumption that I had any medical experience with a species he hadn't even identified.

"Your ship came from the direction I'm told the worms were found, and I did not acquire this one from Lord Zorn, so he would not be pleased that I didn't wait for his return to choose from his own stock. The trader I bought from did not keep his stock in good repair. You can understand I can't trust either to help me, and I've seen one of your kind heal the Hewve Dragon of a similar sickness. But of course, my silence about your involvement with an unclaimed slave is contingent on your own silence about this worm I place in your care."

When we entered an air-locked room, a strange membrane blocked our entry, and the commander tore through it with a stinger extended from his forearm. We entered, only for him to spit on the tear to seal it and tear through another membrane like a containment chamber.

A strange creature with no visible defenses, but of similar build to the trill, lied prone before us. I approached and used a claw to lift its mouth flap open to see it had the blunted teeth of a scavenger that picks the leftovers of other predators, or forages for plants and berries. These creatures had no wings to fly from predators, and no scales, or thick hide, to protect against becoming prey. I pressed against its small claws only for them to bend under little pressure, not even giving the species an ability to defend itself. It was as vulnerable as a bug, and aptly described as a wingless worm.

"What is wrong with it?"

"That isn't my job, that's yours," the commander scoffed in dismissal. "I'll have the estreld female delivered to you shortly, but as long as she is in your care, someone must be with the worm. Bring the medic that fixed the Hewve Dragon, and the estreld is yours."

"I will clarify that bringing my medic does not mean she is yours to keep. I'm not selling her."

His wings fluttered and folded back, disappearing behind him. "As I said before, as long as you have the estreld in your care, your medic will care for the worm."

I understood clearly enough that Belder would be hostage as long as I was with my treasure. Belder would willingly place herself in whatever harm's way to help a creature in need. Prying

27

her from the worm's side would be impossible if she thought she could help him. It did appear to be male by the looks of the appendage between his legs, but I'd met species where gender was less obvious, and females were self-propagating.

"And should your worm be recovered, then our business is concluded. You will leave both my medic and the estreld alone."

"I have no control over whether Lord Zorn has anything to say about your involvement with what is his, but I will not intervene unless prompted to."

That was as good of a promise that I would receive from such an outlaw.

With a smile, I made it clear to him that my species boasted more than just two insignificant fangs—we possessed an entire array of teeth specifically designed to shred through flesh, and my tongue was rough enough to grate against his thick skin if I wished to extend my barbs. A warning not too dissimilar to his own, I replied, "As long as I don't find you've dishonored me, your business is your own."

We were both in agreement, but I wasn't sure he was aware that in my culture, we considered it perfectly lawful to kill anyone who has gone against their word or sought harm against our mates.

He has given me his word that he will let Belder go if the worm recovers, and Belder will be free to kill any of his crew if they do not keep this word. We don't always warn our enemies when we intend to kill them, and Belder didn't have to lift a weapon to end their lives.

I had a feeling they'd find out soon enough that I was not the most dangerous trill of the crew. I pitied any warrior who faced Belder without knowing who we were.

One bite from a trill was all it took to end them.

After contacting Belder and explaining the situation, she was more than agreeable to help not only the worm, but an unknown woman that was tossed to the streets of a barely habitable planet. By sheer luck alone did my treasure find food that was compatible with her digestive system and just so happened to also be considered trash by a species I'd come to understand were called krelins.

I wrinkled my nose at what my scanners had identified the stones she'd been so desperate to gather for herself as being the feces of the Hewve Dragon they'd brought with them. Apparently, they used the creatures as stone and sand processors, and their feces were used for building materials within their hive, and trash compacting during their travels.

It was high in nutrients compatible for a species with high mineral diets such as an estreld. Her teeth were made of crystals meant for breaking down hard rocks, while also making for a dazzling smile.

I grinned at the reminder of how shocked she'd been when I spoke with her, and she gaped at me for a moment before I understood why my scales tightened and flared. Something about her spoke to a primal side of me. Her light green hair was tattered, dirty, and despite her state of survival, she glowed with not merely a light that was inherent to her species, but one that spoke of her fight for life. Her determination to cling to hope tugged at my gut. I had been in a worse state when Princess Klemon found me on the outskirts of the city all those years ago.

Perhaps it was seeing a part of my past in the estreld that made me so feral inside. I wanted to viciously rip through the throats of anyone who stood by and allowed her to waste away without a claw lifted to help. I wanted to tenderly clean the broken skin around the jewels that adorned her body. But it was that fierceness in her eyes that told me she'd kill the one that pushed her so low, and if I wanted to be there to see it happen, I'd have to earn that right.

I didn't care that her species may not be compatible with mine. I surrounded myself with those that lit a fire within me and reminded me that treasures were often thrown away. Reminding me that I wasn't trash. That's what my ship was built on, and it wasn't a secret that my queen's advisors thought of my crew as disposable. I didn't risk our lives for the council or even the Galactic Authority. I did it for the discarded of my planet. The ones with no names that still had hope in their scales.

"Commander Yueril," Belder connected with my comm, distracting me from my thoughts. I kept the line open for her, despite the risks of being tracked or monitored by outlaws. "I'm with the worm you spoke of, and I've confirmed your suspicions. The Solusgors have reached this sector, and the nanotech seemed to work with the Hewve Dragon. It's possible it will work with this worm too, but he seems so fragile. I'm uncertain of how the creature will react to the technology."

"Do what you can. I'll figure out a new bargain if the worm doesn't recover. What is recovery for the few will be sightless for those who are too close," I gave her a solid proverb of reason to manage her expectations and lessen her guilt should her efforts fail.

"In many we rise," she agreed with my proverb for the situation we faced. The worm's recovery may be nothing more than death's embrace, and Belder would not have a creature suffer merely for being a bleeding heart that stands too close to see what must be done.

We were both warriors of the Galactic Authority of Trillume, but we were not monsters, even if our missions fell in the gray zones of morality.

The light above my door buzzed, glowing golden, before opening. I had thought I would have more time between Belder's arrival at the worm's side and when my treasure would come. I reached for my robe to cover my scales. It was more for her own protection than for a sense of modesty. My robes were adept at absorbing the secretions that lubricated my skin and caused varying degrees of relaxation in species that touched us. It was what kept my skin comfortable and soft, but also helped my ancestors in weakening their prey by rubbing against them before they used their claws to flay them, while their teeth tore their meat apart.

"Oh," her soft voice was heard from the doorway as I let the fabric fall back over my chest. My scales flared along my temples when I sensed a change in her perspiration. Her temperature rose as she watched me. A dilation in my eyes had my second lids flicking into place to detect heat signatures, and her body lit up like a star in my vision. Waves of heat flicked from her skin, much more like flames than what I was used to seeing with most species. Even my fellow warriors deflected heat with their scales, and it took concentration to track the heat at their glands, which blended with the natural heat signatures of the ground itself. If we were still enough, and crouched to the ground, we were nearly indistinguishable from another rock.

She was beautiful, and it took resolve to allow my second lid to recede and pay attention to something else besides the way the heat between her legs throbbed like a beacon for me to hunt. I knew my heat sensors were considered menacing for species outside my own planet, becoming nothing but a black void across my eyes that was said to feel like staring into endless space with no stars. My eyes did that the first time I saw her too, attracted to her heat.

I blinked several times to force my second lids to retract, revealing my more approachable appearance of green eyes similar to both our skin tones.

"I didn't mean to," she began, and I waved her concern off with a hand as I bowed to her. I touched a finger to my temple in reverence to the Goddess Lumei, blessing our second meeting.

Belder would consider me reckless to give my name to someone so soon, but it felt uncomfortable to keep it from her.

"On your lips, I share with you the fate of the stars, Treasure. My name is Yueril."

She lifted a curious brow at me like I had said something odd, but I straightened and readjusted my hood to cover my face in shadow in hopes that would make her more comfortable.

"Yueril," she repeated my name, and a shiver ran down the back of my legs, but I was sure to keep my stance steady so she would not notice the disturbance, or the yearning for her to say it again. I gathered comforts for her on the sleeping platform that would, on my planet, warrant the use of acknowledging my name once more, and I looked forward to it.

"Yes." I quickly realized that she must be wondering why I summoned her here, and quickly added, "I would like for you to accompany me during my stay." I groaned, as I was not usually so perplexed about what to say; or so awkward about waiting for another to say something in reply. I continued when she said nothing. "I do not mean to alarm you. I do not assume we are compatible for mating. You have nothing to fear from my company. I merely, I just..."

If she had no fear of me wishing to mate with her, then why was I so fixated on bringing mating into the conversation? I berated myself before I grunted and threw my hand to the side to show the basin of water, fresh clothes and whatever else she should need laid out on the bed. "These are for you. Do with them as you please. I will be outside when you are ready to show me around," I said with finality, and then stormed out before I embarrassed myself further.

I would have to find another opportunity for her to use my name again. As it was, I could not bear the increasing probability that she would dismiss my offering on the merit of thinking I was courting her. The door opened as I approached with a hiss stuck in my throat. Why would it be so wrong to consider me as mate worthy? Some habits never truly disintegrated. I would always be the desert scum that the princess taught to speak and dressed in fancy clothes to hide my feral nature.

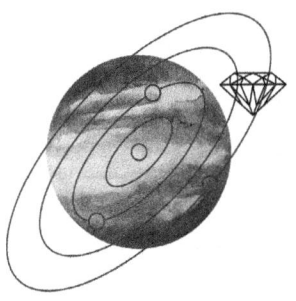

Chapter Five

Hazel

I dropped the fabric I'd tied into a makeshift bag for my food on the ground as I stared at the way his scales twinkled in the light of the room, darkening in coloring as they tapered towards the top of his pants. My eyes lingered on the bulge between his legs and my shoulder loh throbbed as my core tightened and bloomed with heat I hadn't felt since the moons of Estreldez warmed my skin. I shook my head in denial at what I was experiencing, because this was what my mother only talked about briefly when she spoke of my father.

"One day you'll meet a male that sends tingles through your back loh, and warms you like only the moons can. This is the start of mating, and I pray that when you feel this, you will not be forced to give it up for anything," she had warned me.

It was a warning, because I had never met my father, and I had spied on the clan often enough to know many never knew who their father was, and our clan did not allow the mothers to keep their spawn. If you were to look after younglings, you were to take the profession of caretaker where all spawn went, to create a sense of duty and shared responsibility among the clan.

I'd often watched the males and wonder which one abandoned my mother. Which one abandoned me.

The stranger said his name, and I repeated it as my loh on my feet burned where I had cut them out in trade for survival. I figured they were less needed than the ones that absorbed more radiation from the moons, but as my whole body reacted to this handsome male, I realized everything was connected, and needing him hurt so much I believed my wounds would reopen and bleed once more.

He hissed and flung his hand out to show me supplies he had gathered before he rushed towards the door. As he passed me, I reached for him, missing by only an inch before I crumbled. I moaned in pain as my feet ached, and he stopped. The door closed just as swiftly as it had opened. His eyes shifted, and a film covered them as he pinpointed exactly where my loh were missing and crouched down to stare at me with dark vibrating orbs.

"Who did this to you?" he asked with a deep rumble.

I whimpered, unable to admit that this was my own doing.

"Forgive me," he whispered as he lifted his robes over his head and gathered me to his bare chest. His scales were surprisingly cool to the touch, but in a soothing, soft way that had me melting into his hold. I was not a small female, and he lifted me with little effort before placing me on the bed.

My hand rubbed along his chest, and I moaned a protest as he withdrew from me.

"I will tend to your wounds," he explained, and I sunk deeper into the cushions of luxury I had forgotten existed while huddled in the streets against a radiation pack.

I watched as he lifted my ankle and rubbed his fingers along my skin, then... licked my wound. I kicked at him before I could comprehend what was happening. It was a pathetic attempt at shoving him away. My muscles felt like gelatin, and my kick wasn't anything more than a small nudge to him that he easily ignored while he continued to massage my feet.

"What are you doing?" I mumbled, my words slurred. I knew my body was attracted to him and wished to make him my mate, but the way his teeth gleamed as he licked my ankle made me doubt his intentions. Was he going to eat me? My mind said maybe, but my loh tingled more as he touched me, and the moan that was working its way through my throat had nothing to do with pain. Shivers traveled between my thighs, and I felt the seam of my mating loh split as a wetness gathered there.

No, no, no, I repeated. I clearly remember him saying that our species weren't compatible, and he had no interest in me that way. I flushed with embarrassment.

"I'm taking your pain away before I clean your wounds and help you heal."

He was right. My pain was completely gone, replaced with a growing need that made me squirm.

"Are you in pain?" he asked, and I bit my lip at the way his eyes were dark and penetrating. He looked like he would tear someone apart if that would make me feel any better, and he was staring at the one responsible. Me. I had sold my loh. I had caused that pain.

But with him, it was gone.

I shook my head.

My tongue loosened its grip on my secrets, "So you aren't going to eat me?" I asked with a breathiness as my ass slid forward, my foot still in his grip as it gently pressed against his chest, and my lower knee opened, revealing myself to him. An estreld's mating loh only opened when we were ready to mate. It didn't confirm that we were compatible beyond pleasuring each other, but my mother was right about one thing. When the feeling comes, you don't want to let it go.

Would he touch me? He was kind and gentle, and I wanted him to, but I knew this might not be anything more than my body yearning for a bit of kindness after so long of being denied. Would he deny me this?

It seemed likely, just another loss in the mountain of trials.

The scales on his head flared and a mist covered us that made my skin heat as he trailed his tongue up the side of my foot.

His hands were still holding my leg, and I gasped as the sensitive loh at my center pulsed at the smallest of his touches on the side of my leg.

"Tell me what you need," he cooed with a forked tongue licking over his lip.

I needed to feel something, anything and everything that I've been denied for so long, even before I was taken from my home.

Mewling, I wiggled my hips against what I now realized was his tail as it parted my mating loh with careful precision. His eyes were black with what I hoped was a similar need building within him, as his tail grew slick, the more I rubbed against the ridges of his scales. The tip of him pressed in, making me gasp as the girth stretched me as he pushed deeper.

Gripping his tail with my hand, I stared at him as he watched, waiting to see what I would do. My core throbbed around him, and his movement stilled as I held him within me. Quick breaths rasped from my lips as I searched his expression for any signs that I affected him as much as he affected me. His scales fluttered along the ridges of his temple, down his head, matching my heaving chest as I gently squeezed his tail and slowly pulled him out to the tip and then thrust him back in with a moan.

He hissed as his eyes darkened with what I hoped was need, but he did not take control, allowing me to do what I wished with him. A smirk played on his lips as I moved him with deliberate strokes within me until my thighs clenched at the sensation of something fluttering within me. The scales along his tail and around my hand expanded, moving like many little touches, filling and stimulating. My hand had stopped working him within me, and his tail nudged within my grasp, begging me to finish what I started.

My loh jewels glowed, warming in agreement, and I ground my hips up in time with his tail as his fingers trailed along my leg in soothing caresses. His three large fingers reached my hold on his tail, covering my fingers as he helped me thrust in and out in a delicious rhythm.

"That's it. Take what you want," he encouraged. Like setting off the collapse of a star—his deep voice shattered my world as I clamped around his tail and screamed.

A glow erupted in the room from my loh, and I squeezed my fist around his tail so tight I thought I might sever it from the source. My lips throbbed as I ebbed from the flow of pleasure, and he eased his tail from my needy flesh. With a twisted grin, he flicked one last teasing touch to my sensitive mating loh, eliciting a mewl from my throat.

He brought his tail up to his mouth and ran his forked tongue along the length, tasting my pleasure before he groaned with restraint. "What have you done to me, Treasure?"

The reality of what I had just done made me flush with renewed heat. What must he think of me? I was too embarrassed to speak, but then he simply rubbed my legs, and I groaned at how lovely it felt. He took a cloth from beside us and dipped it in the basin of water with his tail, then began slowly washing me with tender strokes.

Salve was placed on my damaged loh at my feet, and as he adjusted his hold on me to have my head in his lap, he used his claws to remove the knots from my matted hair and brushed through the uneven strands as he cleaned.

He continued to stroke my head, and by the time he finished an ache built in my chest that tore me apart. My lower lip trembled, and moisture dripped down my cheeks as my heart clenched over and over at the tender care he applied to my broken soul.

Chapter Six
Yueril

I never saw the appeal of wetting my glands in any warm hole available across the galaxy, and I hadn't considered it a possibility while on a mission with my crew of the Galactic Authority of Trillume. That was something young spawns did before they realized the importance of restraint and the responsibility that came with being a predator species. Yet here I was with my cock glands straining against my scales, and my tail still itching to be squeezed by this treasure's delicious mating oasis.

Her taste was still on my tongue as I bathed her and treated her wounds. So warm. So inviting. Which, of course, she was. I cursed internally at my stupidity. Sulltid, fucking brain bleed;

she was in pain. I rubbed my tincture oil all over her. She was relaxed, and all her pain receptors were blocked so I could help her, and instead, I fucked her with my tail.

Like that was any better than slipping my cock from my scales and wetting my glands with her pleasure. If Belder knew what I'd done, she'd probably challenge me to a duel to knock some common decency into my skull. This place may have been similar to the Blue District of Trillume with its offered companions, but this treasure was not one of them.

She glowed like a star, and the heat from her jeweled skin sunk deep into my scales, making me slow each touch as I stroked the dirt from her pale green hair. I took extra care to be gentle with my claws as I massaged the cleaning powder from her silky strands. I wasn't sure if she was similar to a trill in how to care for her jeweled skin, but I was sure to only dab small amounts of water with the cleaning powder, just in case. Dried out scales were uncomfortable, and using plant oils was not ideal to replace our tincture. Would her glowing jewels be the same?

I had licked her wound on her foot as a trill's tongue contained many antifungal and natural bacteria to promote healing. It is also used to clean our meat as we ate. It was the way our ancestors could eat even meat that would be considered spoiled by other species' standards or help detox the poisonous water dwixes.

I clenched my teeth tightly as I restrained my anger from reminding myself that someone had harmed this jewel and gauged out chunks of her skin like they had descaled my very flesh. I had a particularly rough molting as a spawn, and no amount of tincture could numb the pain of having one's scales plucked one by one.

Then whatever I was thinking vanished the moment I felt moisture on her chin. My claw scooped lightly up her cheek to collect the perspiration that had leaked from her eyes.

What was this, I thought, as her shoulders trembled in my lap? The light from her jewels flickered and dulled, which didn't instill any reassurance in me that she was recovering.

I said nothing, because every warrior I knew would not wish their pain to be acknowledged with words. Words were but awkward attempts at feeling useful in a situation that needed only acceptance. I've done what I could for her healing. There couldn't possibly be a spot I missed when tending to her. I did not leave a single part of her untouched. To my shame, I lingered more than I should have with every soft sigh of her breath.

I held my tongue tightly at the roof of my mouth that begged to have her tell me whose claws I would tear from their sheaths.

Then she spoke softer after a low whimper that broke my insides, shattering them with my lack of a target to destroy. "It was on a rock of tarnpul, overlooking the wading pool, just on the edge of the clan's main palace," she began.

I wasn't sure what she was trying to tell me, but I resumed letting the short strands of her hair play through my claws. Absently, I found myself snipping uneven chunks with my claws, as my own spawn maker would do with the sacred plant she cared for in my youth that spun soft silks from its branches.

"My mother told me not to go to the clan until I was ready to follow their customs. She showed me the way to that pond and spoke to me about how that was where lovers went when they were not sired to each other. She left me there to watch overhead as the couple that was there touched each other.

"It was the first time my mating loh ached, and I rocked myself against the smooth tarnpul I sat on. I guess I haven't learned much since that rising."

I listened as she spoke of pleasuring herself and I ached to be used as she used that rock, as she used my tail only a short time ago. Her head sat in my lap, and she turned, rubbing against my swollen scales that held back my cock to stare up at me with vibrant green eyes. She nibbled on her lip, and I felt the shift in her like she was about to retreat, but I held her face and nodded for her to continue with what she wished to share with me.

"I," she stopped and then took a deep breath and continued, "I went to that pond often, and that was the last place I remember before I was taken. Before I was given to Lord Zorn's ship, and during processing..."

I couldn't hold my words back anymore thinking about her in the captivity of slavers, "They took your jewels?" My muscles tensed like I could jump from this bed and kill them like they were in the room with us.

45

Her eyes were wide, and she shook her head before averting her gaze. "No, one of the slaves helped me leave saying the only thing that awaited me where I was going would be death if I didn't find a way back to my planet. No..." she paused with a whimper, "I removed them myself."

I gathered her up in my arms and we stayed there until her breath was shallow and came in smooth cycles.

Destroying an entire empire of outlaws would harm their slaves more than the low life that ruled them, I reasoned with myself. There would always be the blue market traders that lacked moral navigation in their bones. Striking one down would only ensure another grew in its place.

My brain spun up like an engine firing through the endless space of the galaxy until I realized the answer was already in my grasp. By this time, my treasure was fading into her mind, and I stared down at her with resolve.

"Never again," I promised. She would never again feel the need to trade herself for survival. The pieces were already in motion, with no one willing to claim responsibility when the stars begin to break.

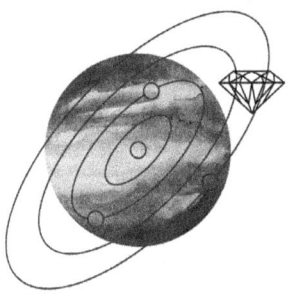

Chapter Seven

Hazel

My body ached as I startled awake with the realization that I had slept without my radiation pack. My loh wouldn't have absorbed enough energy to function properly for the day without it. My lungs burned as I gasped and clawed at the hard wall I was against. My fingers grazed off the firm surface, and a low chuckle rumbled around me as my hands were gently held down.

"To a new rising, Treasure."

"I didn't mean..." I realized with shock that I was clawing at the one who had helped me.

"It'll take more than that to scuff up my scales," he assured with a twinkle in his eyes.

My hand went to my rough throat. "It's just the last time I woke up aching... it was after I was..."

"Taken," he finished for me, and he started to move me away. I clung more desperately, wrapping my arms around his neck.

"No," I begged. He was cool to the touch, but it felt nice against my burning loh jewels. If they didn't have radiation to absorb soon, they would crack the skin surrounding them and I would start bleeding again.

"Are you in pain?" he hissed in question.

I nodded against his chest.

"That shouldn't be possible," he said before he cupped the loh at my shoulder and pulled back, staring at it with narrowed eyes. "My scales disperse heat, but you are burning too hot for my tincture to absorb into your skin. Is this normal for your species?"

I breathed in his scent and rubbed my face against his cool scales with a sigh. "This planet doesn't have a moon. I traded my loh for a radiation pack that I normally sleep with."

"Where is it?" He stood immediately and grabbed his robes, which he promptly pulled over himself and me with his tail, while he continued to hold me to his chest. I was not a small female, tall and lithe like much of my clan. The robes were large, and both of our heads fit inside the ample fabric of the hood.

I giggled despite myself. On Estreldez, our fabrics were thin and light. We rarely, if ever, covered our loh from the moon's rays. Having so much fabric seemed so odd until I came to Delta Fal, where I had to cover my loh just to not bring attention to myself. Many leered at them greedily like I was a walking jewel mine that they wished to pluck the riches from my flesh. I would not survive it.

"Your robes are much larger than even the two of us," I had to explain my sudden outburst, not wishing to offend him. I hadn't noticed how much fabric there was before as the layers folded over each other and I was too focused on his eyes. Well, that and he wasn't wearing it when I caught him shirtless. His tail was hidden until it'd snuck its way between my legs. I flushed at the memory.

"The thick robes protect others from coming into contact with my tincture oil and keep my scales comfortable. The hood is to stop my baser instincts from spraying enemies or ... mates while also hiding my predatory nature." He smiled, showing off his razor-sharp teeth.

He had sprayed me before with a mist that came from his scales along his head. I bit my lip, wondering what exactly the spray did to people.

Like he could read my mind, he added quickly, "If I'm under duress, the spray can poison my enemies but... when I'm mating it enhances pleasure sensors."

"Oh." I rasped with awareness and my mating loh throbbed with an expectation of feeling more of that pleasure spray and something more than his tail.

We were out the door and exiting the Den of Bounty when the junk trader stopped us. I squirmed, unsure of what Yueril would do if he knew she was who I sold my loh to. Not that the old Shol woman knew how painful the process was of removing a loh, or the lasting damage that resulted from it. She was the only one willing to speak with me or trade with me on this planet.

She had tried to convince me to be a spy and figure out what the trill were up to, and she guaranteed that she would find a ship that would take me home if I succeeded.

But a few kind acts from this strange male and I doubted everything. Here he was carrying me to find my radiation pack, and the only thing he asked of me was to hang out with him while he stayed on this barren planet. It could have been anyone. Why me?

The old shol spoke. "I've come into possession of some tarn-pul. From the krelins, highly conductive. Great source of stable radiation! Heat your rations safely. Makes functional jewelry!"

Tarnpul wasn't tasty to eat, but it stored the radiation of the moon's rays and was sure to still have some left in it for quite some time. It's how my clan survived the storms inside the mountains when the moon's rays were blocked by the debris in the atmosphere. I clutched onto Yueril's neck tighter at the mention of it. He seemed to remember me speaking of the tarnpul earlier and asked the trader if it was native to Estreldez. Before she could even answer him, he faced her and said, "We'll take it." Not even asking how much it cost.

The trader handed him a heavy bag, and she gave him a strange hand gesture with her pinky and said, "In many we rise."

"It has been a while since I've been home and heard the greeting. You'll know then what I have to trade and may pick it up from my shuttle."

He dug into the bag and pulled out the black polished rock of tarnpul. A soft glow pulled between my loh and the rock as it got closer to my skin. The radiation sunk deep into my muscles and the raspy wheeze in my lungs eased as I began to process the stored power of the moons. It had been so long, I nearly wept again.

We made it back to the shuttle yard, and I finally got up the courage to ask him, "What do you trade?"

"We trade in many medical supplies. This tarnpul will barely cover the cost of a few vials. The trader knows she owes her boon to you, as the trill have far greater advancements not readily available this far out in the galaxy." He paused and stopped walking before he spoke again, but not to me. "Belder?"

I couldn't hear the other side of his conversation, but his nostrils flared, and he cursed—at least whatever words he said next did not translate.

He glanced at me apologetically. "I must return to the Den of Bounty. Where is this radiation pack of yours?"

Not wanting him to see where I used to sleep, and with the tarnpul so close, I didn't need it right away, so I shook my head. "I can come back for it later. The tarnpul may not be worth much to you, but it will save my life here. It feels like home." I held the rock close to my chest.

"Then you'll come with me?"

I nodded with a shy smile. Yueril still hadn't let me go, holding me in his arms like I weighed nothing. His tail was propped under my butt and wrapped around my inner thigh.

"I don't know what I'm walking into when we return." He eased me down his body until my toes touched the ground. He was only slightly taller than me, but not by much. Our foreheads touched, and he lifted the robe above his head and slipped out, leaving the large garment over me, the fabric now grazing the dirt.

I'd seen the horrors that happened to those who weren't cut out to be outlaws. It was a clan with a deadly admittance. The robe over my shoulders was used to protect others from Yueril, not to protect Yueril from his surroundings. I admired the way his scales shimmered in the dim light of the artificial beams surrounding the shuttle yard. This planet was more like an asteroid than a habitable home, barely in orbit of the nearest star. Its heat source was from beneath the surface.

He handed me the pack of tarnpul, and said with seriousness, "These are yours. It isn't normal for Belder not to respond, which means she was surprised by something... or someone."

A female? A twinge of jealousy heated my cheeks, but I hadn't even told him my name. I enjoyed the way he called me treasure too much.

"Pull the hood down over your face when I tell you to," he instructed, and we made our way back to the Den of Bounty.

The junk trader was nowhere to be seen, and that in itself was suspicious. I grabbed for Yueril's forearm. "This doesn't feel right."

He nodded. "I'd say my crew is being welcomed to the planet with a winner-take-all challenge."

I took a step back with fear and uncertainty. "I've seen what they do to offworlders that try to do business without using their services. I'm only alive because they are waiting for Lord Zorn to come and take care of me himself..." It went without saying that my time was limited to find a way off this planet before he returned, even if it meant sneaking aboard someone's shuttle and gambling where it would travel to, or if I'd get caught.

Borrowed time.

I took a deep breath and a deliberate step forward.

"Treasure," he reassured with a lick along his sharp teeth, "I won't force you to join me, but even if they ambush me, you will be the only one to survive it."

He flexed his claws, and his scales glistened like he was covered in the waterfall's mist from my home planet, and not off to enter a trap on an outlaw claimed rock. Muscles rippled beneath his scales, and a sharp thorn slipped out from the tip of his tail. He could have torn me apart, yet instead he destroyed me in a way that had me smiling at the excited anticipation in his dark eyes.

As we entered the Den of Bounty, there was no guard positioned anywhere to greet us. It was eerily quiet and empty as we moved through the halls, yet Yueril didn't pause to stop as he moved fluidly with determined precision.

He finally spoke. "The rooms are empty."

How did he know that?

We approached a room, and it opened to a torn membrane like entering the stomach of a large animal.

"She isn't here..."

But we hadn't even entered the room before he was turning fast and pushing me behind him.

"I can see you," he said pointedly in front of us, but there was no one there.

A voice from the hall echoed, "It's rare to find a species that is capable of detecting me before I strike." Laughter bounced against the walls, and I blinked several times, uncertain of what I was seeing appear from within the air itself.

I gasped, covering my mouth before I fell to the floor, before the image of Estreldez's Moon God.

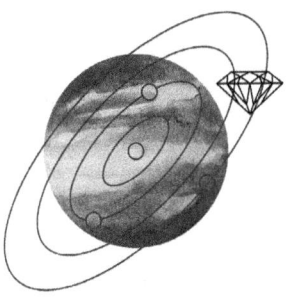

Chapter Eight
Yueril

E very room was empty, but there was a heat signature following me. The blur of heat kept moving, making it difficult for my eyes to pinpoint where it was, so I kept moving. I would check where they kept the worm first to see if Belder was still there. Her scales, like mine, made finding her by heat alone more difficult without being in closer proximity. Checking behind me, whoever was following us kept hiding behind the heat of my treasure, which blurred my vision and left me in awe every time I gazed at her.

Once I was as certain as I could be that the room was empty and my treasure was beside me, it was clear the heat in the hall was not hers but that of the one who followed us. The intense flicker of light made my eyes itch, much more concentrated than the flow of heat from many species. Even my treasure's jewels were like a beautiful flame that dissipated in the air, flickering and cycling through pulsing ebbs and releases that I could stare at for eternity. Mesmerized as I was when she had slept in my arms, uncaring if my second lids would burn or blind me should I find myself staring for too long.

I quickly placed myself between her and the intruder as it approached, hissing in warning through rows of fangs, and flexing my scales with uncertainty as the male's laughter echoed off the walls. The way his body stung my eyes, I knew I could not continue to locate him for much longer without ruining my heat sensors. As my regular vision returned, I squinted and confirmed my suspicions that his body acted much like the deserts of Trillume, creating mirages in the sweltering heat and confusing our sense of direction. My poison wouldn't work indirectly if it burned up before reaching his blood stream, but a single scratch should suffice.

As the mirage appeared before my eyes, my treasure fell to her knees with a gasp at the golden male, and softly she mumbled, "Great Goddess blessed..."

I lifted a brow ridge at the male covered in blades and jewels. His long blond-white hair floated behind him with invisible heat waves, his arms covered in curved blades that sprouted from his skin and spanned beyond his elbow. Large yellow-blue crystals flexed from his shoulders, a fan of jeweled daggers displayed like the ring of a star's rays, much like the treasure behind me.

"How refreshing to know my mate has lied to protect her image on the planet that she discarded me from. Still pretending she is descended from the moon goddess herself, is she?"

I wasn't following what he was saying, but the way my treasure trembled before him made me hiss with displeasure. If he thought she was his mate, he wouldn't be thinking at all soon enough.

He waved me off, but only took a single step closer before stopping again, keeping a safe distance from me to assess what kind of threat I was. Smart. My claws itched to pry open his jaw wide enough that he'd have trouble smirking again before my poison took his life for challenging me, for taking Belder, and for striking fear into my treasure. My posture was straight, and my tail relaxed beside me to focus on what needed to be done.

I was a warrior, and was trained in the ancient trill hunt—before the meat-breeding plants made many of our warriors complacent with the ease of our food from the markets. Once I lured my prey into false security, my close-combat training was all I needed to defeat them. He believed he was powerful and in control of this duel, which served my purposes just fine.

"You've come to be in possession of something that belongs to me, and I've made it a point to prove to my mate that she is no goddess. She will regret the rising she severed my mating glands and took the planet for herself." A sinister gleam glowed in his yellow eyes as he grinned with a twisted sort of resolve. I've seen that look before in warriors that have been pushed too far and lost their minds. I'd had to cull my own warriors in the desert from the sickness. He was not speaking of my treasure as his mate. It was someone else, and he would lash out at anyone that reminded him of her. For a brief moment, I pitied him. If my own mate betrayed me, I would be no different from him. Broken, and my mind twisted.

"The Almder doesn't own the clan..." my treasure spoke up with shaking breaths.

"Does she not?" he asked, bemused by the interruption.

"What does this have to do with me?" I challenged to change his focus back to me.

"You've taken my property, and it costs me fewer lives and trouble to kill you and sell the moon flea for parts rather than to let you go and send the wrong kind of message to those that would wish to take my place.

"You see, it's rare that I get to talk to anyone before I kill them, and a dead worm tells no tales. I plan on ruining the Almder of Estreldez by showing the fleas that follow her how she cannot keep them safe, and one day they will rise up to lead themselves like the very slaves worthy of one day destroying me," he explained with deranged excitement before laughing in warped delight.

"You want to be destroyed," my treasure's soft voice hit the heart of the issue and why this male was so dangerous. He had no fear or moral compass to give him pause.

"It won't be by you, sweet moon flea," he assured. "I've found there are many buyers for an estreld's loh, from merely decoration, to grinding them up and using them for creating more effective clothing to absorb and deflect radiation for species that do not process it well. Even a few use our skin as an aphrodisiac. Beauty and function, the fabric and jewelry, even glow when in contact with radiation. The last buyer even created a robe with radioactive materials so that the loh are constantly heating and glowing for both warmth and glamor. I'll earn a pretty credit from your flesh. And," he paused to assess my own skin, "I'm sure scales such as yours would do nicely as well."

I grinned at him, unaffected by his taunts. "My scales are not for sale, but perhaps you'd like to know what it feels like to have your skin used as an accessory." I flicked my claws against each other to sharpen them. My claws were perfect for flaying flesh, and I felt my tongue barbs push to the surface on instinct that there was a meal ready to be shredded.

The damaged mind of the outlaw before us was merely amused by my statement, uncaring of the real danger I posed to him. The only thing that stopped me in that moment from making him my next meal was that he had similar features to the treasure behind me, and I struggled with whether she would appreciate that eating him would save our skins or if it would forever imprint the image of me destroying something so similar to herself.

I would never eat her... my lip twitched into a smirk, remembering the taste of her sweet release from my tail. At least, not without her permission, I thought as my tail fidgeted behind me. It was a trial to stop it from moving too much when she was so close, but it was an advantage for my meal to forget I had another limb at my disposal. One with a large claw unsheathed for a fight at the end of it.

"There's a reason why the Almder called me a god," he said, while taking a step closer. My scales could feel the heat rolling from his jewels. "My loh were honed to survive from very little radiation and the excess radiation stored in my loh makes it possible to become a ghost of the moon's grace... or vengeance."

He disappeared again in a blur of heat that even when I closed my second lid over, my eyes burned and blinded me from knowing exactly where he was before refocusing.

When I could see the solid heat signature of my prey once more, I pretended to sniff the air like that was how I noticed he was there before and not by sight of his heat. I needed him to get close for my tincture oil to work efficiently in such volcanic temperatures. My eyes were straining, and my second lids wouldn't last long under the extreme heat he was producing. My scales adequately dispersed the extra steam in the air with ease, but my second lids were meant for tracking prey that weren't as hot as the suns.

My tail was still behind me, not wanting to cause undue attention. I moved to the left, the opposite direction of where his heat was focused, showing him my back. I waited for the scales on my tail to dry and swung my tail low, while my head scales misted, and my arms lunged in a rotation. My claw met the resistance of the blade on his forearm, and I clamped down on the sharp weapon, bending it with the heat he was producing until it was melting into his own skin. The heated glow of his loh flickered the longer we fought against each other's hold for dominance.

I took a moment to make sure my treasure had listened to me and lowered her hood over her face so as to not breathe in the mist.

The echo of his laughter haunted my eardrums.

"I'd heard rumors of your kind. Able to resist the radiation heat with your scales, but this is remarkable." His teeth gleamed, though not in a threatening manner I would expect from dead meat. My poison should have been working its way into his system with how close I was.

I showed him my own teeth, rows of razors prepared to shred him. His grip on my own arm seared against my scales, damaging some of my gland production, but his grip was loosening.

His eyes grew wide as he realized what was happening to him. Even without poison... the numbing properties of my oils were penetrating. But he wasn't the only one surprised as we pushed and turned in the hallway. My scales were unable to dissipate all of his heat. Glands were bursting beneath my scales, muscle was heating, yet even I barely felt it as my own grip faltered due to the numbness of my tincture oil seeping below the protective armored layer.

The heat, combined with the tincture oil, was bringing my tissue beneath my scales to boiling temperatures that I knew weren't sustainable for either of us. Steam rose around our movements as I hissed, locking my jaw from a deeper ache in my arms that my oils haven't reached yet.

"Why don't you use those sharp teeth of yours, lizard?" He gritted out, words swollen from the oils that evaporated in the air, making his tongue numb.

I refused to bite him unless it was a last resort. How our poison worked was a secret that kept our species safe from those who wished to challenge us.

"He doesn't have to," a beautiful voice taunted from his side as she placed her hands on the daggers blooming from his back and she gripped them with all her might as she glowed. Her head bowed back as she screamed a war cry that had my heart skipping with a vicious kind of excitement.

The more she glowed, the more the outlaw weakened, and his mouth gaped open before his knees crumbled to the ground. He released me, and I fumbled backward to the wall, balancing with my tail.

She was magnificent as she shone like a thousand suns, burning up the robe that was supposed to be protecting her from the poison in the air...

Goddess, help me.

Would she forgive me?

On unsteady steps, I forced myself to push through the heat and remove one of her hands from the melted mess that was crumbled on the ground at our feet. There was no time for explanation, not that she was fully coherent to accept any words from me. I tried to avoid puncturing any of her precious jewels as I found a space on the inside of her elbow and bit down. I concentrated on bringing my antidote up from my throat as I tasted her blood. Using the barbs on my tongue to scrape her skin to allow more area to accept the counter agent specific only to my poison. Retracting my barbs and spitting into her wound should be enough with the short exposure time. I held her wound with my tongue to give it more time to enter her blood stream before I unlatched. My tail wrapped around her shoulders to keep her up before she fell against me. I made my way out of the Den of Bounty one difficult step at a time to create distance between us and whoever finds that we'd killed the largest outlaw of this sector... Lord Zorn, himself.

Chapter Nine
Hazel

From the moon's grace, a god was crafted from the molten core of our largest moon, Lupa. Skin the color of white and blue crystal. Loh was capable of glowing so hot that no eye could gaze upon the moon god without bestowing his light on those worthy of his blessing.

From his seed, warriors were given his power to disappear amongst the stars. Our loh were not bound to their jeweled form, but burst forth like the wings of a loretig, a great creature that disappeared along with the clan's mythical sky warriors.

But there stood one, a warrior that appeared just like the crystal statue of the moon goddess's gift of a god in flesh to protect our clan. Only the Almder herself was known to have loh that could replicate rapidly with the moon's rays and sprout as the loretig once did. He appeared out of thin air, and I stared in shock as he disappeared like a wave, blurring until there was nothing.

I stared as the scales on Yueril's head flared, and I quickly brought my hood over my face as he instructed. I couldn't see anything through the thick fabric, but I heard the sounds as their boots scuffed on the ground, loh and claw scrapped, and that twisted laugh of a male that marred the beauty of a clan I never got to be part of.

My lip trembled with self-pity as I cowed in the disillusioned safety of nothing more than a thick blanket of fabric. I wanted so badly to be accepted and rejoin my clan, even after my mother's passing, but I missed every chance given. Time and time again, I could have returned to the palace, explained why I was alone, living in a cave beyond the clan borders.

I chose to be a coward then, too.

Yueril hissed, and it wasn't the kind of noise he made as I wrapped my mating gland around his tail and squeezed. It was... pain. I couldn't stand by, crouched on the floor, as he protected both our skins from Lord Zorn. Shame made me hesitate that such an outlaw came from my planet, born from the decisions of a leader I never got to officially meet, and my mother abandoned to keep me by her side.

A lifetime of indecision and I finally lifted my hood up to see it was wrong of me to allow someone else to handle my battles for me. Yueril wouldn't have been in this position if it weren't for getting involved with a runaway slave. Glowing a bright green, my loh burned in preparation. I didn't have the power to transmorph my loh into a weapon like Lord Zorn, but I held firm that he was no god of Estreldez and his energy stores were as finite as the rest of us.

Quietly, I moved behind Lord Zorn, and as he threatened Yueril once more, I leaned in and growled out, "He doesn't have to." I will, I thought wickedly. I will be the one to kill you myself.

With renewed vigor and resolve, I gripped his back loh and began absorbing as much of his radiation as I could. As fast as I could, I pulled his radiation into myself, channeling it into the tarnpul strapped to my hip. Fire coursed through my veins, and my jaw clenched down to stop the scream bubbling up from my throat. I swallowed the pain down as I continued to syphon from Lord Zorn, praying he was too occupied with Yueril to fight back and reverse the flow of radiation back into himself. I felt the jerk of his shoulders as he tried to get away, break the connection, but I held tightly. Blood flowed from my palms, along my forearms, and dripped from my elbows, glowing from vengeance instead of grace, just like Lord Zorn wanted.

The pain was too much, and my head flung back as I screamed towards the ceiling, wishing that the last thing I saw in this world wouldn't be the boring metal of the Den of Bounty.

I always dreamed my last moments would be staring at the moons, showered in their glow as I returned to the ground that gave me life. That wasn't supposed to be today, I thought wistfully, as my energy to hang on drained. I was overloading my loh. I knew that from the way my skin felt like it was melting, being drenched in my own blood seeping from the seams around each jewel.

Still, I didn't let go. I didn't stop pulling the radiation from the male that wished to take my freedom, my skin, my life. My throat grew hoarse, and my screams became silent, though the air still pushed from my lungs in an effort to be heard. Someone hear me... I thought with disappointment that Lord Zorn was winning, even when I was taking his life. My own would follow him into the void.

I felt the flow of radiation weaken and knew I didn't need to continue anymore. He had less radiation in his loh than I did the day I crawled to the trader with the largest loh from my feet dug from my flesh, begging for the radiation pack that saved my life.

Funny, I thought with a smile, as the feeling in my arms tingled and something tore my hand from Lord Zorn's back loh. I didn't even care that I felt my melted flesh tear apart, sticking to where I gripped him.

Lord Zorn got exactly what he wanted. My freedom, my skin and... my life.

Numbness crept up my back and my knees shook from my own weight. Pressure pulsed up one of my arms, but I couldn't see anything through the haze of radiation.

"Forgive me," I heard the whisper of Yueril's deep voice. It was a strong sound, and I smiled, knowing that he would live. As if that confirmation was all I was waiting for, I collapsed and allowed the light to take me.

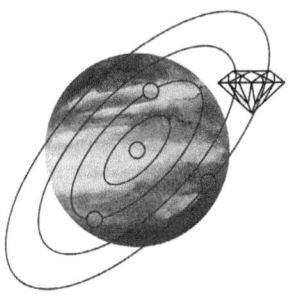

Chapter Ten
Yueril

E very step pounding against the dirt ground felt like lifting a mountain to move us both from the vulnerability of being in the open. I'd made it out of the Den of Bounty, but my limbs were tingling, and my movements were molasses, sticking and making each decision a chore. I needed to make it to the shuttle.

Belder was still unresponsive to my communications, and I couldn't connect with my ship. The signal was blocked, and I knew that was the planning of Lord Zorn to disable any frequencies while he handled his "business".

I stumbled and hissed as a young unGor grabbed for me from an alley between buildings. I couldn't spray him while my treasure was too exposed from her cracked and bleeding jewels. They were a species that respected the Galactic Authority and its laws, but they preferred to keep to their own planet's diplomacy. It was odd to see an unGor this far out in the sector of outlaws. No stranger than finding a new species on this barren rock and one of them being a notorious outlaw that had a whole ring of heartless bastards cowering in fear and compliance. I wasn't fooled into thinking killing Lord Zorn would be the end of things.

"I can help her," the young unGor placated quickly. "You can't return to your shuttle—it's been sabotaged."

"How do you know this?" I narrowed my eyes to slits, untrusting of this out-of-place unGor.

"Because I'm the one that was ordered to sabotage it. Lord Zorn always has someone who double checks my orders, so I couldn't just leave it alone. My brother is the best pilot I know. He can bring you into the hangar of Lord Zorn's ship without being traced."

"And why would I want to do that?"

This youngling was out of his mind if he thought I would bring her straight to the ship of the very male who was responsible for the state we were both in. I didn't trust anyone on the ship to keep her safe when my body finally hibernated to heal. She would return to my ship, not a slaver vessel.

"Because Lord Zorn has a radiation chamber created to simulate the moons of her planet that will help her heal, and a special injection I've seen him use to repair his loh even after near death. He's feared not just for his ruthlessness against those who disobey him, but because no one has been able to kill him. Many have tried."

"He won't be recovering this time," I stated matter-of-factly, and I watched for any signs that this unGor had any remorse or anger for knowing his leader would not be returning.

"Then you have nothing to worry about spending a rotation on the ship before returning to your own. He came in his smaller vessel so your crew wouldn't be on alert. Your warfleet could easily destroy it, but that would alert the other ships if you attacked."

"Why are you willing to help us?"

"Not you, Hazel," he corrected, while motioning his chin to my treasure. "If Lord Zorn knew who she was, he would do worse than kill her, but if he found out after killing her or someone else doing the honor, he would destroy many lives. He is not right in the mind."

Hazel, I thought of her name, and irritation flowed through me that she had gifted this outlaw with her name, yet not once offered it to me in return. It was against her own rights to privacy to use her name without her giving it to me of her own will. I would be forced to continue to call her Treasure until she told me the name herself, but I clenched my teeth together at how this lowlife was granted such an honor. I used my tail to sneak up and wrap around his throat with the claw pointed at his chin.

"You will not use her name on your tongue," I demanded as I lightly pressed the claw into his skin, and squeezed my tail around his throat for a small reminder that I may have been injured, but not incapable. The tincture oil would numb his neck, but not enough to stop him from speaking. I was still too dry to completely subdue him, but he didn't need to know that.

The youngling lifted a brow, and his small braids twitched at his neck. He was too young to use his tentacles to reach my tail and help loosen my hold. The unGor used their hair to hide the appendages from their head, but they've been part of the Trillume Galactic Authority for many cycles now. We knew of their anatomy. One day, the male would grow to have long tentacles that could rival my own tail, though they didn't have any claws or spines in them.

"She is Lord Zorn's offspring," he croaked out.

"How do you know this?" I released my tail on his throat, but kept it wrapped in case I needed to squeeze the life from him.

"He never looks at the medical files of slaves. What's the point if he's just going to send her to be skinned alive? She shares his DNA. He's incapable of having offspring, so I thought it was impossible, but there's no mistaking it. She's from his seed, perhaps before he lost his mating loh?"

"Why are you telling me this?"

"Because Lord Zorn's empire is hers if he is truly dead."

He won't recover from the poison without my antidote. I nodded to the unGor. We didn't have more time to discuss this. My ship didn't have the resources necessary to help a species that wasn't in our database. If I had to wait for her recovery and then escape a slave ship, that's what I would do to save her. She wasn't some outlaw's daughter; she was my mate.

I stilled with this realization. My mate... was that even possible?

Why my body responded to a different species, I may never know, but I was certain this treasure was meant to be mine, just as I was meant to be hers. When a trill bites someone, it's because we are cleaning our food or marking our mates... She'll never be in danger of my poison again if she takes my antidote and accepts my mark.

I had no choice but to claim her without consent, even before she gifted me with her name, to save her from the poison in the air. Would she forgive me for such a sin? Even if she never did, at least she would be alive. I would have to accept whatever punishment she gave, even if it was to reject being my mate.

The unGor tried to take my treasure from my arms, and I hissed in warning. He lifted his hands and grinned at me, recognizing my territorial response for what it was.

"I'm just trying to help. You may still be able to kill me with whatever last strength you have, but I'm not sure if you'll make it back to the bindle grappler after such a display."

I arched a brow ridge at him. Bindle was translating to a different language than what he was speaking... krelin? A destroyer.

"It's a small attack ship with arms to destroy another ship in close combat or dismantle key resources from a larger ship without detection until it's too late. It will get into the hangar of our ship without detection as it wasn't reported as on assignment, so we'll just return it to its spot in the hangar and no one will care. Traded it with a krelin and Vareo took a liking to it."

"Vareo is the pilot, your brother, you are bringing us to?" I questioned, and he smiled with a wave of his arm to continue towards the destroyer ship.

"He will pilot the ship."

The unGor quickly acted to right my footing as I stumbled, and we finally made it to the shuttle yard. Behind a large pile of broken ships and trash was a ship smaller than a traditional shuttle, but larger than I was expecting of a stealth ship called destroyer.

What stepped out of the open door was even more surprising. This was not another unGor, and he was half my height. I hissed at my escort and expressed my disagreement with this arrangement, "You think I will let a spawnling control the fate of my mate's life?" The unGor wasn't much more than a spawn himself, but this male standing not even chest high was beyond unacceptable. He couldn't have been old enough to know how to fly a ship.

"I'm more than capable, reptile," the boy snarked while cracking his knuckles with a smirk before turning his attention to the unGor, "You sure about this, Gen? Lord Zorn won't be happy that we kept this information from him."

"According to the trill, Lord Zorn is dead. Even if he isn't, we'd be in more danger if we let her die."

"I guess," Vareo said with a shrug. "Load up then. We have to be quick to get this thing back to the loading bay before communications are active again."

"Lord Zorn won't kill us for disobeying him, you know that," the unGor reassured the spawn with strange marks on his forehead and neck. The bird burn behind his ear was recognizable as the same one I saw on my treasure's ankle. A mark of a slave, I thought with growing anger.

"We might wish we were dead when he's through with us. He better be deader than the last time."

They both looked at me for affirmation. "He won't recover from my poison without my help," I assured.

They both sighed in unison like they were of one breath. As young as they were, they seemed to have lived more life than most, and I nodded with understanding. I would trust our lives with these spawns that hold a depth of age their years did not account for. I had no choice in the matter. I would hibernate soon to recover. Whether or not I woke again would be up to them.

The destroyer had two sleeping bays, one on each side of the ship behind the piloting deck, and a small cargo hold that would barely contain enough supplies for any long distances. Certainly not a large enough vessel for being able to make it to the nearest planet without the assistance of a larger ship.

As the ship thrusters lifted jerkily, I also noted the destroyer was not meant for landings or takeoffs planet-side. Its design did not lend to smooth navigation under the atmosphere of the magnetic pull from the planet's core. Using my own body, I shielded my treasure from jostling too much as she had to be strapped to the small cot barely large enough to hold us within one of the rooms.

We made it into orbit, and the unGor entered the small space as I adjusted upright again. He held out a medpack from my own shuttle supplies. I could tell by the mark of the Trillume Galactic Authority emblazoned on the film protecting the adhesive applicator.

"Use this until we get there," he offered.

Taking the medpack, I immediately applied it to Hazel's thigh with delicate precision. Medpacks worked best when applied where there was a large artery to transport the nanobots and support replicating for a faster healing process. There was no telling if it would work well with her species. It was untested by Trillume's scientists, but it was all we had at the moment to help her last until we got to Lord Zorn's personal medbay.

"It'll work to help stop the bleeding. Lord Zorn has used them before," he assured, sensing my uncertainty. A wise youngling. He held out another medpack, but flooding her system with nanobots wasn't going to help. If anything, too many nanobots could be dangerous. It was best to wait until these had a chance to work and be flushed out of the system.

He added when he saw I wasn't reaching for it, "For you."

The younger one with markings came up behind him from the direction of the pilot deck and shook his head with a grin. "You look like shit. Listen to the big guy and take your medicine or we might be eating lizard for dinner."

I nearly laughed, but measured my features at the youngling before staring at him with a serious expression to see if I could make him flinch. "Eat me, little bandit, and you'll join me in the beyond unless you have a tolerance for trill poisoning."

"Not yet, I don't," he challenged, and I grinned at him. He reminded me of myself as a spawn. A bit reckless, but eager and determined to grow strong. I took the medpack and applied it to myself. They were right. I suffered severe internal damage from my oil glands rupturing beneath my scales. The medpack would help, but I would still need to hibernate to shut down unnecessary functions and regenerate broken tissue. The medpacks technology was invented by a scientist that was able to replicate the regeneration properties of a trill after losing a tail or hand. We were very difficult to kill, which was why I was even more frustrated with myself for not handling Lord Zorn more efficiently, so Hazel wouldn't be in the state she was in now.

Hazel, I repeated her name in my mind and hoped that she would grant me the honor of saying it out loud by offering it to me when she woke.

"We'll be at the ship in a parcel rotation. We didn't dock at the planet, so you wouldn't see us coming."

"Did you take any of my crew with you?" I worried about Belder, though I shouldn't. She was perfectly capable of regenerating if they harmed her. Most species believed we were dead when we simply went into hibernation to heal. Our heart beats were imperceptible, and we already ran cold with our scales deflecting heat. As long as they didn't dispose of her out an airlock, or damage her heart, she'd be fine, I assured myself.

I went to pace the room, but a soft hand clenched in my claw, halting my retreat. I stared at the beautiful treasure before me and cringed with agony at how blue blood was leaking from her lovely jewels. Blue covered her soft green skin, leaking from the cracks in her deep emeralds. A moan whispered from her lips.

To give her something else to think about instead of the pain, I began to tell her of my past, "I was raised on the outskirts of the city where I had to train, as my ancestors had, to survive among predators of beasts with no thought other than to consume and roam the deserts.

"By my own clan's standards, I was nothing more than an animal with no rights to join the clan and more respectable beings of the universe. My whole crew is made up of animals tasked with protecting the planet when those of higher respect curled their tails in distaste, but I was willing to sacrifice myself and everything I knew to secure a future for them."

I shook my head at the oddity of speaking to a female that could not hear me. And even then, I was lying to myself and to her.

With a sigh, I corrected myself, "To secure a future for Princess Klemon. She was the only one who came to the outskirts dressed in her lab cloak and saw the life we lived as our ancestors had before us.

"She was there to test a new nano technology on unsuspecting animals, but she didn't. She kept returning rotation after rotation, bringing comforts of the city with her until I decided to approach." I could feel my neck heat with the memory of embarrassment at how I had acted then. "I had fully intended on mating her as she was beautiful and kind. In those days, I didn't think that she would turn me down as I was the strongest of the outskirts, regularly providing leadership and food for the rejected ones. We did not realize we were rejected ones at the time. Without words, I was similar to what you would call a savage warlord of the desert."

Her eyelids fluttered and fingers squeezed my claw more forcefully as she groaned out, "Mine."

I smiled, not even thinking about if I appeared frightening. Perhaps she could hear me in her dreams, and it warmed me deep within my cartilage that she felt the connection between us as I did.

"Yes," I agreed. "Yours, My Treasure. She was not my mate, but she did teach me the common tongue so she could ask permission to install my implant. Funny, how a basic language understanding is necessary for the functionality of the technology in our minds, as the program must have a base-line language to associate with or communication is pointless even if it translates many languages across the universe.

"Even us talking now is all made possible by our implants communicating with each other. Princess Klemon taught me the civility of our clan and tasked me with joining the Galactic Authority. I took her experimental technology.

"All of us did," I added with a sadness, thinking about my crew... and Belder.

"What does it do?" she whispered, and it allowed my muscles to ease, knowing she was conscious. Though her eyes remained closed. The medpack was helping, and the spawnlings didn't have to heal us at all. This small act was comforting as I felt my eyes close from the numbness seeping through my muscles.

"It stops foreign DNA from attaching to our cells," I explained. "But it's untested against the threat it was created for.

It seems to have been proven to stop the replication of foreign cells in our bodies. The nanobots have saved countless lives and improved countless others from disease and death. But against what we face... the Solusgor, we cannot know for certain until the threat reaches here from Solunus.

"That is why we are here. The side effects of the technology are unknown. It's only been used on the dying, and on my team. We must know that the threat is neutralized and that there aren't any adverse effects from prolonged exposure to the Ganpan-Fal in high doses. That is our mission."

Instead of fearing about what was to come, she said, "Solunus was destroyed..."

"No," I corrected her, "The planet still exists. It just doesn't belong to the Shol, or even the Galactic Authority, anymore."

Chapter Eleven
Hazel

"Do you think he's dead?" the youngest outlaw asked. When we were boarding, I saw he had the same kind of markings the shol trader had.

"Unlikely," the unGor who had helped me before replied, Genbi was his name. "From what the lizard said, Lord Zorn was alone when he attempted to handle business himself. Lord Zorn is never alone. It's likely he had the whole den at his disposal, and there were insurances in place should something not go according to plan. This is probably a lesson he has planned for you, Vareo."

Genbi helped me escape before, but from what I was hearing, I wasn't sure if he'd do the same for a second time. There was a kind of respect to his tone when he discussed Lord Zorn. If Lord Zorn is never alone, then someone would have recovered his body, and if they were loyal, then they'd be making efforts towards healing him. He may not be dead after all, I thought with a shiver that made my limbs ache.

"Like the incident back on Sumtraliaq?" Vareo cursed under his breath. I continued to lie strapped to the cot in the opened room next to them. There was no door to this room, only a curtain that swayed with the air vent below it. I had a feeling this wasn't always a room outfitted with bedding. The cushion between my body and the hard metal slab was thin, and the straps appeared more for cargo than for transporting a lifeform.

I stayed quiet to see what else they had to say when they believed we were both unconscious. Yueril was slumped half on the cot and half off, with his head resting on my stomach and his tail wrapped protectively around my leg. He stopped talking in the middle of a sentence, and I couldn't even feel his chest move with his inhale of breath. He was cold to the touch, and I would have thought he was dead, if it weren't for the way his tail periodically pulsed around my calf. The conversation echoed through the vent.

"I wouldn't doubt it," Genbi agreed.

"Sumtraliaq was a blood bath. He sent unprepared slaves with no warrior training to a planet with barely any land surface.

They were eaten alive, and the ship was lost!" Vareo grew more agitated with every word. There was no love lost from him towards the Lord Zorn. That was my only comfort, that I might be able to trust them long enough to get back home.

"And what did he say to you after?" Genbi prompted.

"It was an investment in the future," he scoffed. "To have the ship send back information about the resources and species there, but also to monitor when the species is capable of using the ship to their own advantage to communicate with the galaxy. He sacrificed all of them."

"Now that planet is under Lord Zorn's jurisdiction. Anyone who trades goods to or from that planet has to pay their dues. It is Lord Zorn's right to do so after paying the fee in blood and lost goods."

"The bastard is not right in the head."

"He doesn't take from the planet; he takes from those that wish to use the planet. That is one of the lessons. The lengths he goes to strike fear into those that would oppose him is but a method of controlling how much is taken. When you're older, you'll understand that the slaves that follow him don't stay because of any fear they have of him, but an understanding of what he is building."

"Okay, fucker. What am I supposed to learn from this, then? That we sacrifice some slaves for the lives of others? And when am I going to be the next sacrifice? What then, Genbi? What then? I'm nobody's sacrifice! And what right did Lord Zorn have to decide on who gets used and who doesn't?"

I felt a twinge of familiarity with his words. Was I nothing more than another sacrifice?

"Vareo," Genbi said with a chuckle. "Why would he teach any lessons to someone he plans to sacrifice?"

My lip curled up in distaste as Genbi's image in my mind warped from savior, from a life as a slave, to that of a male that couldn't be trusted even temporarily. Whatever kindness he showed me was to meet his own ends, and I might simply be another lesson for someone he did care about. I tried to reach the release button on the straps that held me down, but it was near my feet, and the metal latches were facing the opposite direction that required more of a push than a pull action, even if I touched it.

"Plans change, Genbi," Vareo said with a growl.

They certainly did, I thought, while smiling fondly at Yueril. He was in this mess because of me, and I'd find a way to get us both out of it. Somehow. I tried to melt the metal at my feet, my teeth gnashing at the pain of even trying to use my loh when my largest ones were torn from my flesh. It was no use. I whimpered as I felt moisture drip down my heels from fresh blood where my wounds were reopened from my efforts. It hurt, but it was tolerable with the numbing oil from Yueril's tail wrapped around my leg, seeping into my skin. I had to wonder if he knew I'd need it, and that's why he curled his tail around me before his eyes closed. I closed my eyes and groaned at the way my consciousness was fading to join him. We would be at the mercy of two outlaws that were at odds about their opinions towards Lord Zorn, and inevitably towards whether they would risk their lives for ours if it came down to it.

"Then what's your plan?" Genbi sighed. "It won't take long for the crew to know something happened to Lord Zorn. Now's your chance to escape this life, if that's what you're looking to do."

"You won't come with me." Vareo understood what he didn't say.

"No one truly leaves Lord Zorn. The experience buries itself inside your very en. One cannot live in the light without a bit of darkness."

"My en died the rising my planet was destroyed."

But if he was shol, then he wasn't alone. There was a whole colony of shol beneath the surface of Delta Fal. His planet may be gone, but his clan was not. I'd tell him as much, but I couldn't be sure of his loyalties. I wouldn't be responsible for exposing the last of a species to the largest outlaw organization in the system. The tincture oil from Yueril was no longer being burned off by my radiation, and I felt the numbness travel up my limbs.

The intercom across the small ship crackled to life. A woman spoke, "Vareo, I know it's you. You're the only bastard stupid enough to take a ship for a joyride the moment Lord Zorn is busy."

"You going to tell Lord Zorn?" Vareo snarked back.

"No need," the woman replied flippantly. "He already knew you would. Why do you think it was so easy for you to leave?" She waited a heartbeat before haughtily continuing, "What? You thought he didn't notice when a ship was decommissioned after being repaired? Why he favors you, I don't know, but now that you're back and the hangar is closed, I'll connect you with his comm. Like he requested."

I struggled to stay awake to hear what was happening, when the last words I heard were, "Vareo, my son, did you recover my lost moon flea?"

Lord Zorn...

Tapping rang through my ears, waking me with a startled gasp that I choked on through a mask forcing air into my lungs.

"There she is," Lord Zorn's voice was muffled, but distinctly his. "Did you know that fleas aren't that much different from any other species? They survive off of another's life force, the blood of another."

I struggled at the sound of his voice, but found my shoulders bumped into warm metal and it felt like I was floating. With a blow of air out my nose, there was something suctioned around my face, but I couldn't open my eyes yet.

"Oh, don't get me wrong, little moon flea. Being as we are the same species, being a flea doesn't have to mean you spread disease wherever you go, like those that follow the one you call Almder. Fleas may not be able to fly, but they can jump one-hundred and fifty times their own height. To their fellow grounded fleas, they are gods that soar the skies. They also have an endurance stronger than many others, able to sustain activity for thousands of jumps without rest, if they tried. Are you a disease or a god, little moon flea?"

My voice was garbled behind the mask, but it was there as I replied hoarsely, "You're the only one spreading disease across the universe."

He chuckled like I was being cute. "A disease, or freedom? Depends on who you ask. I was prepared to pluck your flesh while you slept, but my son told me something curious enough to change my mind."

His son, that was the second time he said that, and the last time he was referring to Vareo. Was the young shol part estreld?

"You see, the healing pod you're in was designed for me, and only me. My DNA. And seeing as you are now awake, and healing nicely, we both know the implications of such a thing."

"How are you still alive?" I changed the subject before he tried to say something ridiculous, like he was my spawn maker. My mother told me that we lived separated from the clan because of her love for my father, and wanting to raise me herself instead of with the clan caretakers. Lord Zorn was a god of myth that hadn't been seen in the clan for many rotations before I could have possibly been spawned. It was logistically impossible with him running his slave empire to have visited Estreldez during that time.

"Now, or back when my mate betrayed me?"

I didn't have the words to respond, so he continued without them. "We'll start from the beginning, my progeny. You see how your color is so pale compared to the vibrant colors of your peers? I didn't think much of it before, but when I was a youngling, I too had such a pale complexion. It fades more as you age, until your hair is white, and your green skin is no better off. The blue of your oxygenated blood will seep through the layers and become a blue-yellow tinge until you look like the ice of the southern mountain range, farthest from the moon's rays. Your mother's green eyes will stay, though. My eyes were always golden."

My mother didn't have green eyes...

"You don't know what you're talking about," I gritted through clenched teeth as I struggled within what I now realized was some kind of gel liquid.

He tsked with his tongue. "Your mother lost many offspring. Not a one of them lived for longer than a few risings. But what many forget, my precious jewel, is that she wasn't the only one with loss. They were mine too. My offspring torn from my grasp as they burned too hot too soon, falling to moon fever before their loh were developed enough to survive. I had enough. Every offspring, she would harm herself further by removing a loh from her flesh. Try again, another loh would be removed, but bigger, more brutal of a sacrifice for each subsequent loss. I was losing more than an offspring each time. I was losing my mate slowly. Any further damage and she may have soon found herself unable to take in the moon's rays at all."

He paused then, and I barely pried my eyes open to see him watching me through thick gel and a viewing window to the healing pod I was in. His loh were still shattered, blue blood was still dripping down his flesh as he slumped in a chair, hooked up to tubes and a soft glowing light. I had injured him more than his voice betrayed. Lord Zorn appeared exhausted and near death while he spoke of the death of his offspring, and the woman who was obviously not my mother. My mother had all of her loh intact.

An intrusive voice in the back of my mind reminded me of the stories of the Almder herself, and how her very crown was made of tarnpul and her own flesh. It was adorned with several loh that much of the clan believed were from her offspring as a reminder of her loss, and perhaps the smaller ones were, but the larger ones would have been impossible to have come from a new offspring. As much as I hated to admit it, his story fit with what I knew of the Almder, the leader of Estreldez.

Lord Zorn continued, "I met with the medical staff to discuss ways of preventing any further offspring, and that was the rising she betrayed me. She had the medic subdue me as she removed my mating loh. I woke up on a ship, in the middle of nowhere, as I was being sold on the blue market to an outlaw on Sholonus that planned to gore out my loh to save her clan. She was under the impression that the radiation in my skin would burn out the disease in her mate. Her mate didn't last long enough for her to return. I considered killing her when I woke, but she wasn't alone. Vareo was with her, and I strangely could not leave him. He was mine. Everything in me said he was mine.

"Mine to protect, just as he is yours to protect as well."

I didn't understand what he was rambling on about. Mine to protect? After losing so many offspring, he must have snapped.

"As my daughter, you must carry on my legacy and protect the future of Estreldez through the shol. They are the key. The markings on their skin, they aren't fleas like us. They are the moon, not a parasite of it. It will take centuries to build up their population, but we must find another female shol to bond him with. When their numbers are stronger, we will integrate them with estrelds and the offspring will be cured. Future estrelds will rise from fleas to the gods. No longer beholden to the moons. Just being near a shol is like being near the moon's rays."

"I'm not your daughter," I said while struggling within the medical pod.

"Your mother knew I wouldn't let her continue to try for more offspring when she was destroying herself in the process. I thought she was punishing me for betraying her need for progeny, but she was taking what she needed and removing the obstacle towards her goals... me. Your mother's stubbornness is what I loved about her, because it meant she stopped at nothing to achieve great things."

"My mother had blue eyes," I objected.

He didn't even acknowledge what I was saying as he continued, "Don't get me wrong, I still have every intention of destroying her for what she did to me, but I have to admit that without her betrayal, we may never have found the solution to the moon sickness, or the increasing amount of estrelds with smaller, and decreasing number of loh. The clan relies on the Almder to help them absorb the moon's rays and mate. She uses this as her way of staying in power, but she knows that without offspring as strong as her, she will be the death of the clan. Reliance makes us weak. With the shol that will all be in the past.

"It's up to us, my jewel, to make sure Estreldez has a future. With you, and the power you showed at the Den, you can lead the clan to a better future. We must diversify our offspring to ween away from the dependency of our moons. The moon sickness will become a greater threat in the coming centuries. Our entire clan could become extinct if they cannot survive the darkness as the moons pull farther away. The moon's rays will become hotter and the dark side will become colder. Smaller loh could mean death for our clan. The tarnpul can only do so much. And we have bigger problems approaching our sector that may destroy our very planet, just as Sholonus was destroyed."

It was a lot to take in. You'd think I wasn't talking to the most notorious outlaw in the sector as he spoke of saving planets and preventing extinction.

His voice was ragged, exhausted as he said, "I don't tell many people this. I can't, because my reputation depends on not having reasons for what I do besides protecting my profits... my business. Revenge is the only thing I allow the universe to see. The darkness I must commit is all I allow them to see. Like your mother, I am a stubborn flea, unwilling to stand by and watch as my clan unravels. Sacrifices must be made, and I'll do whatever it takes to make sure there is a future... even if that means I must be the darkness that allows the light to be seen.

"Rest now, my jewel. There is much to do before you take over as Lord Zorn."

Take over?

"You've lost your mind," I choked out. The mask over my mouth and nose filled with a thick scent that smelled of burning metal and my eyes grew heavy as my muscles twitched.

"Genbi," he called out. "Prepare the airlock with the trill. We'll let my daughter do the honors of ending him after she wakes."

My heart sped up, thundering in my ears, but all that did was speed up whatever drug I was inhaling, and my mind was filled with nightmares of Yueril's body freezing before it explodes as I watched. Space was an unforgiving place, and I'd seen the same happen to a slave that launched himself out the airlock rather than being sent off to who knew where. He didn't have the same help that I did in escaping. I'll never forget the horror of that moment when I realized every slave died... it was just a matter of how.

I wouldn't let Yueril's story end in such a horrific way.

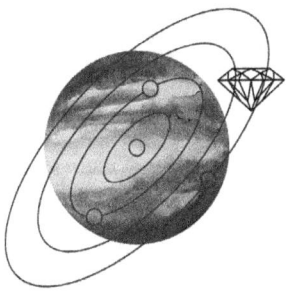

Chapter Twelve
Hazel

As I felt the fog from my brain fade, I heard Genbi's voice, "Her vitals are stabilized..."

"But?" Lord Zorn could tell there was something he wasn't saying.

"But, her loh are damaged. She was weakened when she attacked you, and according to the tests on her radiation absorption, she will have to be returned to Estreldez sooner rather than later. She isn't holding onto the radiation like before. If you remove her from that chamber without being near the moons, or a radiation pack, she won't survive. She will have to live on

Estreldez for the rest of her life, possibly carry a radiation pack with her in case of any disruption from the rays."

"She won't be capable of being the face of the Birds of Zorn..."

"No, My Lord."

A loud crash echoed through the chamber as Lord Zorn cursed. I would be lying if I wasn't relieved that he wasn't going to force me to be part of his outlaw organization, but a spike of fear made me wonder if he would really let me return to Estreldez... or if this was just another reason to kill me. I had no usefulness to him, even my loh were not worth extracting for sale if they couldn't hold radiation. He'd be better off throwing me out the airlock and into space like debris.

Time went by in silence until I finally processed that even if I lived and made it back to Estreldez, I would be an outcast. I've never lived with the clan. None of them knew me, and I would be reintroduced as someone who was damaged beyond repair. Self-pity almost made me ambivalent to whether I lived or died.

Lord Zorn whispered into his comm unit. His voice echoed through the mask I wore within the med tank. "I'll find a way to fix this."

The sound of footsteps told me he had left. I opened my eyes and saw Genbi staring into the med chamber, startling me.

"Don't worry, I didn't tell him you were awake," he began. "I'm assuming I don't have to repeat myself by telling you that I can't remove you from the chamber without risking your life."

I nodded. Whether Lord Zorn knew I was awake was the least of my worries. I was more worried he'd come to his senses and realize I was of no use to him alive.

"Good. I'll also say that it's unlikely Lord Zorn will give up anytime soon. You will not be returned to your home planet."

That truth stung worse than I thought it would. Why would I have any expectations that my estranged criminal seed giver would do anything as kind as return me? But there was that brief moment of hope that he would act as any other spawn maker would. Warped hope as it was, I knew better than to bet on it when I hardly knew if he'd keep me on the ship or kill me.

"Why are you telling me this?"

"Because I know you don't want to be the next Zorn of the birds, but I also believe that you should know that he is correct in at least one thing."

"What is that?" I snarked. I doubted Lord Zorn had anything of value that didn't involve destroying someone's life.

"That you could be the one to discover another way to help your species and the birds. We all can. Why live your life struggling to survive rising to rising, when you can be free to make real change? You will be stuck in this medchamber for some time. What will you choose to do with it? Be a victim and waste away? Or tell me what you wish to learn, so you can do something when you are able to leave?"

He was brain washed by Lord Zorn, and I knew well enough that it wouldn't matter what I said to him. He wouldn't bring me back to Estreldez without Lord Zorn's say so. What could I do while stuck in this pod?

The reason why I was stuck here was my loh.

"I want to know how my body works. What makes it function? So that I can fix it myself."

"Interesting..." Genbi considered my request. "Fixing yourself wouldn't change the predicament you're in, would it? Would leaving the medchamber change things?" He shrugged, leaving me to think about what it would mean to be fixed, but still stuck with Lord Zorn.

Would fixing myself simply put me in a different sort of cage? Genbi stopped as the whir of the door opened with an exchange of air between zones. His voice could be heard echoing in my ears, "I'll have the security commander acquire a scientist that might know more about it. I'm sure Lord Zorn has probably asked her to do that already, though his reasons are different from yours."

Many risings passed before someone visited again, at least while I was awake. Even then, it wasn't to see me. Alarms blared through the room, and Lord Zorn pried through the door, shoving it into the hollow part of the wall on screeching metal. The room must have been locked down, or some security breach made it impossible for even the Lord Zorn to enter without force.

There was nothing I could do while stuck in the medchamber. He didn't even glance my way, like I was merely decoration in the room as he darted straight for a panel in the wall. He tore it open and slammed the lever down. The siren stopped, but the flashing lights remained. Blue haze filled the room like it had its own heartbeat. Screens filled the wall, showing an array of halls and rooms throughout the ship.

One in particular caught my attention. It was the airlock Yueril had been in, and it was empty.

I didn't know if that was something to be relieved about, or terrified. Had he removed Yueril from the room to be jettisoned from the ship? Or was he moved somewhere else, keeping true to his word that I would be the one to send him into space?

Lord Zorn enhanced a different screen with his crew shaking and convulsing on the ground while the sound of retching could be heard. He tapped the comm unit and commanded a passing warrior to move them to medbay. They hesitated before dragging the bodies off the screen down a different corridor.

"Isolate the infected. There is nothing that can be done once they've reached this point. Prepare the decontamination sequence for the locked down sector," Lord Zorn commanded.

I didn't hear what was said on the other line of the communication, but Lord Zorn's irritation made it seem as if the person on the other side did not agree with him. "Once the infected have been isolated, burn off the sector."

Chapter
Thirteen
Yueril

"Leave him," I heard a voice say as my scales itched from being overly dry. It was typical for that aching feeling when hibernating in a place not in ideal humid conditions. Memories of where I last had consciousness were in the hands of outlaws and the hope that they were able to finish what I could not. Keeping my mate alive.

"The virus doesn't breed in the dead. No need to bother moving it to the incinerator. Grab the emergency oxygen converter and prepare for the decontamination sequences for this sector."

"There aren't enough hazard suits for everyone in this secto r..."

"Then they better hope they don't touch anything contaminated until the medics come to clear us."

"You're right," they replied with uncertainty.

My tail twitched as the feeling returned to my limbs. I wasn't fully healed. I could tell by the way I felt more heavy than like the refreshed feeling I got from recently shedding my scales. That was the last stage of recovery— completely reforming new scales and the dead scales molting away. My skin felt tight, too tight. I was waking early, which was rare.

Ancient warriors used to die in the wilderness if their tribe didn't protect them during hibernation. It was risky allowing us to become so injured that we risked this deep state of unconsciousness. What would have triggered waking me early?

My heart beat faster than normal, speeding up the recovery of my consciousness and the ability to move my claw tips.

"What was the first sign to watch for again?" One of the strangers asked with a shaky voice that pitched up at the end, nearly missed if you weren't hyper focused on only a voice.

"The medics said the virus heats up someone's insides and makes them itch until they either pass out or tear their own hides off, like they are trying to extract the virus externally."

"Right," his voice quaked. "Itching."

"You aren't feeling anything, are you?"

"N-no. You know I get anxious about these things. Just thinking about someone else itching makes my talons ache."

"Get out of your head and let's move to the next room so we can get scanned sooner than later."

"Has anyone survived the virus?"

The other male didn't reply, knowing once the virus latched on, there was no one who lived long after. By the time anyone noticed the virus was around, it would have been breeding long enough to be very near the end of the incubation period. If they were talking about the Solusgors, then the only hope would be a direct injection of nanobots and hope it wasn't too little too late. The countervirus I was in charge of unleashing on Delta Fal was more of a pre-emptive measure that was untested, and if we were on Lord Zorn's ship, like I suspected, then their ship wasn't exposed to the nanobots yet, at least not in enough concentration to help.

Where was my treasure?

The Solusgors were here. Did my team arrive in time? Only myself and Belder were directly injected with the Ganpan-Fal. The rest of the crew were exposed to it at the same time as the rest of the planet. Would it be enough when the virus was already here?

Great goddess... we might be too late. My skin was tight. Too tight. The dryness of my scales was acutely annoying and begged for my claws to dig into them. That was normal, I assured myself. It was natural to want to molt old scales, but my new ones wouldn't be ready to protect myself if they didn't come off on their own.

Screams echoed outside the room from the hall. I groaned and forced myself to move. The whole playing dead during hibernation wasn't going to save me if the Ganpan-Fal didn't block the replication of the virus. This was my job. This was my purpose. I had to make sure I was in contact with the virus to truly know if the nanobots worked.

Stumbling to the door, through what looked like a storage room of waste product they'd dispose of on the planet. It was a myth that anyone actually polluted space regularly. Tossing things out of the airlock is a last resort. Waste is best properly disposed of on-planet for recycling and decomposing. Or sometimes, an incinerator, but even that costs valuable resources best utilized elsewhere on a ship. It wasn't uncommon for species unfamiliar with the trill to be unable to detect our life signs while hibernating.

I moved my tail back and forth to help get feeling back, and felt like I was back in the deserts of Trillume with nothing but my wits and skills to keep me alive. My robes were gone, my pants were melted into my scales in areas from the radiation damage of dueling Lord Zorn.

I could sense the heat signatures in the hall, and when the door wheezed open, I could hear the other male's sobs. "I had no choice. I couldn't let you die like that. Forgive me..."

"Th-thank you," the other wheezed. I now saw he was a rare species from a planet under the control of Lord Zorn. He had light green skin like some trill, but unlike our own scales, his seemed so delicate and he had long braided blue hair and fleshy flaps on his arms that flared and fluttered. There wasn't much known about the planet other than they were too primitive to have reached space without interference, and there was very little land, making it extremely inhospitable for most species to invade.

Blue blood dribbled from his neck gills. Ah, that made sense. It would be more difficult to keep air-borne viruses out if his gills never sealed up outside of water. A bulge grew on his neck and pulsed. The other male didn't seem to notice as he held him in grief. I knew making myself known would only distract him further from what was happening. The host was dying too late. If he was already feeling itchy, the Solusgor was already formed enough to be released.

The other male might have been informed enough to know of the threat, but not enough to realize he needed to incinerate the victim at this stage. Killing him would only release the creature early. The head was always the last thing to form. It was also a Solusgor's weakness when they came out. Too freshly made to be hardened yet.

I had to approach them both slowly, yet not wait too long for it to infect his friend. They were the most volatile after first consciousness.

The male continued to sob, and the bulge in the dead pushed the other head to the side more. This one was foolish to linger. I was close enough now to spray them both. It should stall the Solusgor as well as prevent the other male from accidentally helping the thing escape from its host. I sprayed at the same time the male retreated enough to see the bulge in his friend and scramble back. I was dehydrated and didn't have any tincture oil on my scales to help incapacitate either of them. The male bumped into my shins and I wrapped my tail around his neck to stop him from fighting too hard against my poison.

I could always give him an antidote before he dies, but the first side-effect of my poison taking hold was nerve damage, enough to help freeze up his muscles. I squeezed on his throat and then shoved the tip of my tail into his mouth to speed up the process. He gagged, scratching at my scales with his talons for me to release my hold. I moaned at the relief of a few scales tearing away. It felt good having the pressure ease up where he thrashed.

"Once I secure the Solusgor, I'll check to make sure you aren't infected and then give you an antidote."

His body went limp, and I dragged him back before releasing him to address the threat in the room. Chopping off the head while it was growing would only delay the Solusgor. You have to wait until the head is completed and the growth activation is over; I reminded myself. It was tempting to claw at the head as it pulsed all vulnerable, but the body was fully formed underneath, and the head would simply grow back if you cut it off too early.

I'll give it to the other male that killed his friend. At least with the host dead, the Solusgor is required to grow a new head, instead of using the one already provided.

"What should I do with you?" I asked out loud.

"Leave him," a voice over the intercom said. "The whole sector is compromised. If you touch him, I won't tell you where to go to be scanned for the virus. Lord Zorn ordered the whole sector to be burned. We both know you'd survive that, and I'd rather make sure you don't escape without making sure you aren't carrying one of those fuckers."

"You have scans capable of finding it before it reaches this stage?"

"We keep the exposed isolated for a rotation. That's long enough to see the formation of the extra nerve endings that start to grow and attach to the brain. The medic said the virus creates a new nervous system first, one that allows the host to control the newly formed parts until it's ready to control them itself. But don't think I didn't overhear your little chat with Hazel. I know everything that happens on my ship, and you're going to come with me to go get your little anti-viral bots from your ship and save my crew before Lord Zorn destroys them, or I'm going to make sure something happens to the medpod when I kill Lord Zorn and take over the ship."

The young shol was full of fire and determination. I didn't doubt he would throw himself against any threat if he thought it would help his situation. He was reckless, but if he stayed alive long enough, he would surely be a great leader with such passion to keep his crew safe.

He was already better than me. My whole leadership was designed to sacrifice myself and my crew for the sake of saving future crews from this very situation.

"Lead the way, small fire starter."

"I'll light your tail on fire as I cut it from your ass if you fuck us over," Vareo threatened.

"Your original threat was enough motivation," I deadpanned, thinking of my treasure still recovering in a medtank.

"Make your way to the West entrance, towards sector Pal. There is a utility hatch in the guard station that only opens when both sides are unlocked. You'll open it on your end, and if you pass the scan from the guard station, then I'll let you out."

"I haven't been exposed for as long as the rest of the crew in this sector," I pointed out the fact that the scan would mean nothing.

"Even if you're fucked, if the scan can't detect it, then we have enough time to get what we need and return. If you care about your mate, then you'll help me, and come back to be scanned again."

I nodded. "True enough." He's already heard my conversations with My Treasure to know I've bonded, and his species had a strong mate bond that his youth would sway his logic enough to believe others held the same connection with their own mates. I would have to remedy that belief after we retrieved the reserve stores of the Ganpan-Fal. He wasn't wrong about what I would do for my mate, but there were plenty of my species that would not do the same.

I reached the guard station relatively easily with the help of the young Shol that redirected his crew that held respect for him over the intercom ahead of my arrival.

"If you don't mind my curiosity, how are you doing this without Lord Zorn's interference?"

"He disabled his own access to this sector the moment he considered it lost. He may be ruthless, but he doesn't want to watch his crew die, even if he was the one to order it. He'll simply monitor the sensors as they go dark from being incinerated. Lucky for you, one of our best security commanders was on his rounds and got stuck in that sector. He doesn't want to be incinerated, and he believes I can do what I said I could."

"What exactly did you promise him?"

"That I've seen a beast with the sickness be cured with the supplies from the trill ship in port, and I'm the best bandit around. No one will approach the sector to verify beyond the sensors for at least a full red-star, and until then, Klaundis will systematically trigger the sensors and then disable them. We'll have the time to get your cure and allow it time to work before evacuating the sector onto shuttles for them to disappear. Then we'll burn the whole sector and no one will be the wiser."

"For a spawn, you have thought this through."

"Fuck you," he lashed out, knowing that I had not expected him to be so prepared. "I may not be mating age, but my species takes over a hundred cycles to mate because we only bond once in a lifetime. Since my species was destroyed, my ability to mate is a useless marker of my maturity. I'm probably older than you, lizard."

"Ah, are you already fifty cycles?"

"Fuck you," he spat again, making me grin. That was a 'no'.

The scan in the guard's room beeped and flashed red. I sighed in relief. Red was good.

"You're clear," he grumbled. "Go open the hatch. It's hidden behind the wall panel. Just lean into it until it clicks."

Following his instruction, I was able to locate the manual seal he spoke of. It required me to release a pressure sensor deadlock. It was not designed for creatures with only three fingers. With a sigh, I angled myself to use both my hands to place pressure in the grooves, attempting to move the locking mechanism. Due to the separation of my thumb from my other two fingers, I had to apply both my hands and then even my tail had to wrap around the grooves to prove I had full intention of opening the hatch.

Who designed this ship? Who had that many fingers?

"Good, you found the glove. It's moving on my side," Vareo grunted.

The glove? I refused to admit to this spawn that I hadn't looked for a device to help other species open the hatch. I was willing to break this vessel through brute force.

"This hatch is fucking thick," he said with a strain that I felt myself as my arms flexed to move the weight of the wheel.

The next forced tug on the hatch finally moved the gears enough to hear the wheeze of released air pressure between the sectors. The force of it swung the hatch open, and I realized that it wasn't merely thicker. The crawl space was surrounded by a volatile compound that, if it combined with a certain rock, was highly corrosive.

Vareo was on the other side, watching me stare at the inside of the hatch.

"Lord Zorn doesn't mess around. If you try to break free of the sector without help from the other side, it would burn you alive and destroy the hatch in the same action. Some have used their strength to tear through hatches before. They didn't make it to rip open the other side."

The force of the pressure releasing made the hatch swing out. My face was covered in the spray of the jelly inside. If we activated the trigger for the rock dust that made this jelly turn to acid, then I'd have been liquified on contact.

I quickly made my way through and quickly closed the hatch before asking, "What about the hatch on the other side?"

Vareo smiled. "They are on the same gears. When I close this one, the other will screw back in place without any help from someone else. Only needs one person to close it."

I saw him wearing the glove that had an extra thumb. Vareo looked down at my own hand to see I was not wearing one and his grin widened, but he wisely chose not to speak of it.

"Let's get out of here before the camera cycles through this area," he said before tossing me a crew uniform.

"I hardly think that will hide being the only trill on this ship."

He laughed, doubling over. "That's priceless. You think Lord Zorn hasn't recruited trill over the star rotations? He's a collector. Sure, there are only three on this ship, and Lord Zorn doesn't trust them enough to do anything important, but I doubt he's the one monitoring the cameras right now. He'll be on damage control." He adjusted the ring in his nose, an air synthesizer. "Here." He tossed one at me that I caught in the air. I attached mine and nodded that I'd follow his lead.

The uniform was tight, but everything felt tight with my scales damaged, and my tincture oil dried out.

An eerie feeling crept up my scales at how easy it was that we were reaching the shuttle bay with no incident or even passing another crew member. Vareo could feel the unease in the air, and slowed down as we got closer to his ship.

"I trust you've thought things through, but I've never seen a ship this silent."

"Fuck, no, you're right," Vareo groaned and pulled at his hair before he paced in a circle. "This is too much like the first time I ran away, and Lord Zorn was waiting at the docks with Genbi looking all guilty next to him."

A slow clap echoed along the large hangar space.

"You're growing up, my son." Lord Zorn's voice made my scales flex up to prepare for spraying the area. I knew that would also include Vareo, and I carefully calmed myself to relax my scales back in place. "Where do you think you're going with what is clearly my property?"

I flashed my teeth at that comment. He did not own me. Lord Zorn merely grinned at me and tapped his inside bicep. I found myself turning my arm over and glancing at my own to see the brand where my scales didn't regrow. A black bird stared at me, and I paled at the audacity to brand something he thought was dead. Or maybe he knew I wasn't, if he had other trill here?

"Don't bother trying to remove the mark," Lord Zorn dismissed my growing agitation clear on my features. "I don't use ancient branding techniques when someone joins the birds. Vareo can tell you."

Vareo snarled, but said nothing.

"No?" Lord Zorn shrugged and picked a piece of dead skin flaking from his shoulder around one of his cracked loh. He was worse off than I might have expected from a male that re-emerged from the clutches of death's grip more than once. He shouldn't be alive at all, but if he were as invincible as others claimed, then still being clearly injured was encouraging for the upcoming confrontation. The ship was within reach, and the only being between us was a male that may have been standing, but I could see the way his limbs shook. My poison was clearly still in his system.

My grin returned as I gave my own shrug of ambivalence towards my new mark.

"Even if you cut your skin and muscle off, the mark will return. It's ingrained in your very DNA. I guess... if you were desperate enough, you could chop off your arm, but I believe your species regrows such things, and it would still be there," Zorn explained.

It didn't make my smile falter, because it would simply be a reminder of the male I conquered and freed my mate from. I was already enjoying the idea of keeping this mark for a very, very long time to come.

I wasn't the one dying today.

"You think I wouldn't notice the lack of resources depleting from incinerating a whole sector? Triggering the sensors was smart, I admit." Lord Zorn smiled at Vareo fondly before continuing. "I'm proud of you, son. You simply didn't take into account temporarily adjusting the sensors for our supplies, or even the drop in oxygen that should have happened if the sector was on fire. Next time, I'm sure you'll plan more carefully."

It was like he was excited for Vareo to one day best him, and think enough steps ahead to outsmart his master. They weren't the same species, so Lord Zorn couldn't be his genetic spawn maker, but there was a twisted fondness there that I couldn't deny.

"Fuck you!" Vareo lashed out, and his fangs were on full display, while an eerie blue glow emanated from the young shol.

Lord Zorn's eyes widened with awed excitement. I stared at the youth, and my second lids slid over my eyes to watch the way his energy grew. Shocked and horrified, I watched as the blueish heat was being sucked along a current—rushing towards Lord Zorn in waves. My eyes retracted back to normal. With his arms extended wide, Zorn's maniacal laughter filled the air. Instinctively, I took a step back. The longer he was in contact with the energy coming off of Vareo's fury, the more the cracks in his loh were healing.

I couldn't believe what I was witnessing, but I suspected that Vareo was the reason Lord Zorn was surviving my poison and the overload of radiation from Hazel. Did he know what he was doing? The anger appeared much too raw to be that of a male who was trying to help heal someone. This was why Lord Zorn kept the youth so close. It had to be.

The male was fast as they clashed together. Vareo rushed Lord Zorn, fangs and claws out with a battle roar echoing the shuttle bay.

Lord Zorn's laughter haunted me as I tried to keep up with them. My species was not that fast. We utilized our oils and spray to disable our prey, slow them down, and knock them out.

I thought of spraying Lord Zorn to help the shol warrior, but I'd only hurt both of them. There wasn't a way to use my spray and only harm one. Or was there?

I quickly removed my borrowed uniform shirt and wrapped it around my head like a hat, closing up any gaps that I could. My scales lifted and sprayed the fabric, soaking in.

There was little time that the poison would be most potent before it would neutralize in the air without a host. Unwrapping the shirt, I re-wrapped it, using the arms to tie it around my tail. My barbs extended from my tail to secure it further.

Lord Zorn didn't even view me as a threat in this battle, merely an observer in his fight with his son. It was just a game he was enjoying torturing Vareo with before he would return me to captivity, and resume his task of burning down his slaves.

Vareo had his claws dug deep into the estreld's gut while laughter reminded the youth that for every injury done to Lord Zorn, his own strange heat was healing him. They were both distracted with themselves to notice me come up behind. Vareo was glaring into his master's eyes. Lord Zorn was chiding with an amused tongue cluck. Neither of their exceptional hearing would hear my approach among their own loud heartbeats and raging tempers. I slowed my own blood to less than what most species would deem alive.

"Why?" Vareo demanded.

"We can't afford to risk the spread of the virus, you know this. The birds know of the risks, and the consequences of not following protocol when returning to the ship."

"No," Vareo gritted back. "You can wait. There's a cure."

"My poor son, it isn't just about saving them from their mistakes. You know this. They've grown complacent. That's why good birds are already dead. You think they should live after being responsible for ignoring my rules? For putting the entire crew at risk? They failed and the rest of the birds will learn how costly disobedience is."

Vareo saw me hovering with my tail slowly readying to strike. A slow smile lifted his lips and his eyes turned black as he allowed his anger to simmer enough for his blue, glowing runes along his arms to fade.

"Whoever was responsible is likely dead already. What you're doing is murder, not justice, and not even revenge. You, Lord, are no longer a bird of Zorn. You've flown too high to be one of us anymore," Vareo said with venom, and gave me a nod.

I wrapped my tail around the Lord's throat and shoved the shirt at his mouth to let the poison soak in. Vareo growled as he lunged his weight into his claws to dig farther into Lord Zorn's gut.

Voices over the intercom chanted from what I assumed were birds from across the ship. "One of us. One of us."

Blood dribbled from Lord Zorn's loh as his body shook and convulsed. We both stood there until the last twitch faded from his cooling body.

"Perhaps this time, we should make sure he doesn't pray for more blessings from the goddess," I suggested.

Vareo forced a chuckle. "I hear the incinerator is great for unwanted viruses."

I found myself releasing the tension in my shoulders with a laugh before I redirected back to the mission, "If you have access to this ship's command, it would be quicker to connect with my ship and have them bring it here."

Vareo nodded, an uncomfortably tight line replaced his smile. He tapped his comm and commanded, "Genbi, connect with the lizard's ship."

"One of us," the intercom continued to chant.

Genbi's voice was heard from Vareo's personal comm, "As you command, the voice of one will be honored."

"Fuck off," Vareo snapped, but there was a small smile barely imperceptible.

The sooner we got this infected sector injected with the Gan-pan-fal, the sooner I'd know whether it worked, and ask my treasure if she'd join me in retrieving Belder, and deciding where our final payload of the nanobots would best be distributed.

Chapter
Fourteen
Hazel

I watched the monitor with relief as the last bird of Zorn was released from the medbay quarantine. The Ganpan-Fal worked...

Many died from the virus, and many would never truly be the same. The virus, Solusgors, was already too far along, and their physiology was completely altered. The only thing kept was their own consciousness.

"Are you sure it's okay to allow them to leave quarantine?" I asked Yueril. "Their bodies aren't their own species anym ore... Only their skulls are the same. Their DNA is warped forever."

The host skin was peeled off if they were too far along in the process, and what was underneath was something entirely different. The skin was hard like rock, and a strange purple which I knew was simply a color associated with a Lightwave that my eyes couldn't process between the red and blue waves. The color didn't exist on Estreldez, at least, not that we've discovered. Nothing reflects between those waves within the light of our moons. It was simply the best way to describe such a phenomenal sight.

"It's unlikely they'd be able to reproduce, or infect some-one else at this point," he explained.

The medic agreed, "Everyone with any signs of the virus has had their mating organs removed for extra precaution, but scratches, blood transfer, and even biting have been test-ed by volunteers that wished for someone who was infected to be released."

I nodded. "The nanobots don't seem to replicate beyond the host, though, at least not without a blood contact."

Yueril agreed, "They can't replicate without a host."

This was disconcerting. "You'll need more of the nanobots to defend against the virus. They don't replicate outside a host, and once they've been absorbed and depleted from Delta-Fal, then you're relying on blood transfers and future spawn carrying the nanobots."

"It's not perfect," he admitted. "But it seems to be working."

I didn't know the solution yet, but I couldn't let it go. Vareo awkwardly forced himself to get riled up to activate his runes like he was preparing for battle once more. He was doing that in bursts to help heal my loh, which miraculously was working. Genbi said I'd be able to leave the medtank soon, but they still didn't know how long the effects of Vareo's radiation would last. They reminded me that even Lord Zorn was requesting Vareo's presence several times while he was recovering.

Something about the shol species reacted well with estrelds.

"We're approaching Krelis," Genbi announced.

The damned krelin ship had already departed from Delta-Fal before we could do a recovery mission for Belder, Yueril's second in command.

"And you think she'll be there?" I wondered out loud.

"The human was meant for the queen there," Yueril reminded us all. "They'll have wanted to keep her to tend to him if anything went wrong. She wouldn't have left someone in need. It's likely she went willingly. We'll know for certain if I get in range of her comms. It's on the way to Estreldez, regardless."

He lifted his hand to the outside of the medtank and smiled sadly at me. I lifted my own hand and pressed my palm to the surface between us. We hadn't discussed things between us yet with everything that's been happening, but I knew he was worried. He swore to me that he would stay on Estreldez if I wasn't able to live anywhere else.

I grinned to myself with the thought that I was sure the Almder would have something to say about that. There were things I had to discuss with the leader of my planet after seeing the results for myself from the medic. Lord Zorn, or Ordin, as was his rightful name. The Moon God depicted in monuments, and the namesake of the Ordin rock deep in the mountains of Estreldez. It was more casually referred to as the glorbin flower after being the favorite food source of glorbins, but even those little annoying creatures were in some respect named after Ordin for being friendly and capable of burning off their food in self-defense, making themselves temporarily invisible long enough to be out of reach. They became clever enough to disappear and steal your food right from your mouth if you don't chew fast enough.

I learned that the difficult way, living outside the clan near the mountain, but I'm sure a few of them made their way into the clan occasionally. Not including the few times I purposefully baited a few to do so when I was younger.

According to Ordin, Almder was his mate, and I needed to know if she was my genetic spawn maker. If she was, then did my mother take me from her? Lying to me my whole life... Or maybe she had sent my mother away after realizing that I was not hers?

I really didn't know the whole story, and though I held resentment towards my mother before this, no matter what I found out, it wouldn't change that I loved her, and she cared for me until her return to the great rock.

"Where is your mind at?" he asked carefully.

"I might not be accepted on Estreldez..."

"It's likely you're the leader's spawn there," Genbi added. "Lord was convinced you had her features, even though you do not have her loh coloring."

No one on the ship called him Lord Zorn anymore since Vareo sent him back to the rock. It was as if, by his end, the title of Zorn was stripped from him. Who would take his place, I didn't know, but there were curious glances aimed at everyone in this command room from who they may see as the previous leader's heir stuck in a medpod, the ever devoted second-in-command Genbi, and the two warriors that defeated him in a duel, Vareo and Yueril.

I knew he wasn't a god of my planet, but I still believed in every estreld's return to the rock, though his would be more in spirit than body. There was no discussion in this room that convinced me what the future of the Birds of Zorn would look like, but not a single bird addressed anyone as the Almder of Zorn, future lord, or otherwise.

The prospect of discussing my future with the birds was more appealing than thinking about whether the Almder of Estreldez was my spawn maker. My mother who raised me was certain I wouldn't be welcomed in the clan, and that would mean she was certain the Almder wouldn't accept me. I refused to think she lied to me about something so serious and still kept the secret on her last breath back to the great rock.

Everyone was staring at me now. Genbi hadn't asked a question, but by the looks of things, they had expected some kind of response to his theory about my genetic connections to the leader of my planet. That would, of course, make me an heir to guiding the clan's future, and either make my reunion to Estreldez a prominent one that could benefit us or a target for being destroyed. It's just as likely my mother was correct in not being wanted and I would be rejected before ever reaching the farthest moon, Bina.

The planet was easily protected against unwanted visitors with the strong radiation fields around the many moons.

Finally, I spoke, since no one else would, "Even if they test me to confirm the claims, I don't want to be the next in line as Almder of Estreldez. I've never been part of the clan, and I wouldn't even know how to do such a thing, but we should consider that making any claims of being the Almder's daughter could result in an outcome we aren't prepared for. If Ordin was telling the truth, then the Almder is capable of dark things."

"All leaders are capable of dark things," Vareo said while pacing in front of the monitors. He appeared nervous and exhausted before he groaned and slammed his fist into the wall. Then he stormed out of the room.

"He knows that he can't go with you. One of our vessels isn't responding to our communications to inform them of what's happened," Genbi explained. "It's one of the slave ships, and from experience, it means someone was dumb enough to take advantage of its smaller crew to steal from us."

"You're dropping me off," Yueril acknowledged with a nod that he would be on his own to find Belder down on the planet Krelis below.

Genbi smiled. "Not without your own ship. Though smaller, it will do fine enough to get from this planet to anywhere within a few cycles. It also happens to be of the same make the krelins use."

"Capable of landing on their planet without suspicion, as long as we locate where to land," Yueril agreed. "My crew will take it from here. In many we rise, I give thanks." He returned his attention to me and grinned. The sound of suctioned air and water gurgled in my ears as my medtank drained.

The mask around my mouth unclasped and snapped back into the tank wall. Strands of light green hair clung to my face without the weightlessness of the tank's gel. I hadn't thought about how much it'd grown during the long periods of unconsciousness, but it reached below my shoulders in an uneven mess.

It wasn't until the front of the tank began rotating to open that I panicked because I hadn't used my legs in so long. I feared I'd fall flat on my face.

125

Yueril kept his eyes on me through the viewing panel, and I locked on as he carefully unlocked the bar I leaned on. His tail wrapped under my arms, and I blushed at the first real touch in several cycles that brushed against the side of my breast. He seemed to understand why I turned my gaze away, and whispered, "There is a saying from my tribe to the Goddess Lumei; on your lips I share with you the fate of the stars. There are three times in a trill's life that we use this phrase."

I wasn't sure where he was going with this, but I enjoyed the way he used his own tongue and then translated it for me. With my legs free from the medpod, he wrapped his arms around me, pressing my damp flesh to his robes without a care for how the evaporating gel should stain his fabrics. Though fabric was the last thing on my mind as I felt his hard scales beneath, wishing that there was no such robe at all between us. Fluttering wisps of air breezed through the top of my head as he cradled me to him.

"When we give someone our name, in respect we say this so that we may meet again to use our names with honor when spoken," he continued. "When we take our last breath, we say this to join the ones we love in the fabric of the universe."

My lip trembled at that one, and I was beginning to suspect he was telling me that this would be the last time I saw him, and not a hope we should say our names together again. That he would go down to Krelis and not return.

"And the third," I prompted.

"This one we save for only our mates to remind them that they hold our first and our last with them always. Treasure," he nuzzled into my hair, and then tilted my chin up to meet his gaze, "on your lips I share with you the fate of our stars."

My loh ached, and my shoulder blades tingled as I stared up at him in awe. I didn't know much about his species yet, but if his fate was on my lips, and my fate was on his, then I didn't want our lips to part. I leaned in and closed the distance to kiss him. He flinched, and I wasn't sure if I had done something wrong, so I stopped in confusion.

Yueril's lips were pressed together tightly, and he too appeared as confused as I was.

I blinked.

"I'm sorry, I thought..."

Genbi spoke up then, and I remembered we weren't alone. "The trill don't normally use their mouth for anything but eating, being as they're full of sharp teeth. You're probably the first being to ever attempt to get that close and not fear being poisoned."

Oh, I thought with a blush. Before Yueril could react, I wrapped my arm around his neck and ran my fingers up his scales along his head. Already I could feel the oils along my skin relaxing me and making my flesh tingly and sensitive. I smiled wryly and watched as the uncertainty in his eyes shifted into something more instinctual.

I was bared to him, fresh from the medpod. It wasn't something I used to be self-conscious of when on Estreldez. Many of our clothes were breathable and hardly more than gauze to allow the moon's rays to touch our loh. Not much was left to the imagination as to our bodies being exposed, but on Delta-Fal... while hiding my identity and what I was meant for, I hadn't felt the stare of another since he'd washed me at the den. My cheeks flushed at the memory of his tail being worked inside my mating loh. Heat pooled between my legs, and I clenched my thighs, wiggling slightly for the friction.

I didn't care if I was making Genbi uncomfortable. On Estreldez, the clan didn't shy from listening to their bodies and I'd seen other couples pleasure themselves, among others doing the same at the dipping pool near the mountain. Back then, I was the one hiding and feeling shame for doing so. The shame I realized wasn't from what I was doing while I watched. It was from the hiding, because I didn't feel the slightest shame for the way I shivered at the way his robe rubbed against my nipples, or for being exposed to more than one male.

Though I'd hardly call being held by Yueril being exposed with all the layers of robes that covered us with his arms around me.

I had no fear that Yueril would harm me, only that he wouldn't do anything at all.

With deliberate slowness, I leaned in again. I stopped, but a sliver away from our lips touching. "Your fate is on my lips; I'd like to give you mine on yours."

A trigger snapped within him, heavy air chuffing from his nose with his restraint, before I gently pressed my lips to his. His shoulders lifted with tension, unsure of what he should do with a strange creature like me that played with a predator. Claws lifted up my back and into my hair as he pressed his own lips to mine more firmly.

His tail wrapped around my thigh and lifted as he hissed and my back slammed into the wall, with his arm taking the brunt of the force of his increased ferocity. The tip of his length curled and slipped between my legs, making my hips rock to warm my mating seam. But I found that it was already wet and ready to stimulate the bundle of nerves within. The oils on his tail's scales heightened the feel of him against me, and I moaned into his mouth. Yet, he made no move to remove his cloak between us.

I tugged at the layers of fabric and lifted and clawed at them. I didn't have sharp nails like he did, but my point was made that I needed more of him. A whimper escaped when I realized he would not give me that minor concession, and I didn't know why.

My eyes closed as I sucked in a sharp intake of air at the thickness of his tail dipping into me. I panted and moaned, using my arms on his shoulders as leverage to move my hips to take more of him.

His tail grew thicker as it sunk deeper, no longer tapered, and I realized that was as far as my body would yield to his tail, yet it hardly seemed deep enough as I clamped around him and squeezed. A shiver of pleasure rippled up my back and made my arms tremble. Heat grew within my loh, and I heard a rough scratching of what sounded like rock against rock behind us, but we were against a wall...

My eyes opened, and I saw Yueril's eyes darting around and then back to stare at me with this look of pure stunned awe. "Blasphemous are my eyes for I have seen a treasure greater than the goddess and I have no care to worship any other."

Embarrassed, I leaned my head back against the wall, only to see from my periphery that my loh had come out beyond their sedentary state. I was glowing all over, and my back loh were sprouted to shards, like lethal daggers spread out like a dangerous flower that framed behind me.

Before I could say anything about it, and what that meant, his lips were on me again, capturing my breath. Back loh were connected with a female's mating. I may have been resentful of my mother, but she had taught me that much. She said, I would know, and my back loh would tingle as my eggs dropped for the right male.

My lips quivered as I kissed him, and I smiled as I pressed our lips together with more passion. Different species or not, he was the right male. I pulled and gathered the back of his robe until I could lift the ends of it over his head from behind.

"I'm okay to simply enjoy your pleasure," Yueril insisted before I could tug the fabric over his head.

"Don't be selfish," I said before nipping at his lip. I had blunted teeth for grinding rocks, but his lip beaded with blood. We both paused, and he grinned.

"I didn't know your species had those," he lifted a claw to tap one of my teeth. I stubbornly yanked the robe over his head for the mass of fabric to gather under his chin and lifted my fingers to my mouth. I flinched as a fang pricked my finger.

"Neither did I..."

"I'm glad," he finally said.

"Why?" I wondered, and he eased away to remove the cumbersome robe between us, and I sucked in my own lip at the sight, accidentally nicking myself, a small dribble of blood tracing down my chin.

"It is customary for mates to mark each other, and there would be no way that your teeth would have been able to before."

I blushed.

"Mates," I tested the word, and he wiggled his tail inside of me, making me pronounce the 'm' elongated as I sunk into the feeling.

"If you'll have me."

I nodded quickly before I pulled him back and nuzzled into his neck. His arms wrapped around me, and I felt a flutter of scales against my cheek and the pulse of his artery beneath.

131

Turning my head, I saw how his scales shifted just beneath his ear. I traced the area with my lips, pressing a kiss there, and he shivered. Was this where mates bit each other?

"When aroused, the scales shift," he confirmed.

I smiled against him and dragged my teeth over the sensitive scales, and he held me tighter until my fangs sunk into him. As I stilled with this heady sensation of fullness and an ache that wasn't being satisfied with his tail alone he gently gathered my arm from around his other shoulder and kissed my inner elbow before his sharp teeth bit down.

I flinched, expecting pain, but feeling nothing but complete.

We stayed there like that for more time than I could focus on. Neither of us unlatched as my hips slowly regained their movement and began to pleasure myself on his tail.

He hissed without releasing his hold on my elbow. "No." He released his tail from inside of me, and I whimpered at the loss. I heard the fall of fabric as what I assumed were his pants crumpling to the floor. My heart felt like it stopped with the anticipation, but I couldn't bring myself to stop biting his neck to look. His tail wrapped around my leg and tugged my feet apart before it caressed my ass and something firm pressed against my mating loh that I knew was not his tail.

He moaned, and I felt his tongue lap against my elbow, sending tingles up my arm. I gasped as his cock pushed inside, and felt so very different from his tail, smoother, but also hitting my nerves in a delicious way that begged for him to give me more.

132

I wrapped the heel of my foot at his ass and pulled him closer to me, moaning as his cock sunk deeper. He was now as deep as I had taken his tail and yet it didn't feel like enough, and he seemed to think the same as he thrust inside of me to his hilt in one sweep of his hips. I tensed up before I relaxed into it, and the tip of his cock hit something inside me that made me shiver and still—unable to move.

Slowly, he eased his teeth from my inside elbow and licked at where I felt my blood drip, but still there was no pain. Warmth spread from the mark, and I released my hold of his neck. My breath coming in deep ragged, barely controlled pants.

"Do you feel it?" he asked with a bit of a worried tremble in his tone.

His cock throbbed inside of me, and I couldn't describe the way the fullness and completeness felt as it utterly consumed me.

"Treasure?"

He never called me by my name.

Finally, my tongue could move again, and I whispered, "When I milk your seed from your pleasure, you will call me yours, and you will be mine."

The worry faded from his eyes and his scales flared from his head with what I now understood was not a threat, but a mating display.

Yueril pulled out slightly and plunged back in, making me call out to the stars themselves as he hit me so deep, I didn't

133

believe it had anything to do with his cock at all, but something intangible as I quaked against him.

Chapter Fifteen
Yueril

I t shouldn't be possible for this to be more than pleasure, but every instinct in me made me bite her again. This time with her permission as my anti-venom coursed through her veins, making sure she'd never be harmed by me for as long as we wandered the stars.

My tincture oils made sure she wouldn't feel the bite, and as my anti-venom worked through her, feeling returned to her limbs and she started to rock herself against my tail. Heat rolled off her in waves as her loh glowed, but what made me stop her from shuddering upon my tail was the way my cock engorged.

It wasn't that I was hard for her, and eager to please that gave me pause. It was the way my sacks filled with fluid and felt heavy beneath my glands. It could only mean one thing... The blood from marking her was activating my need to mate, to fill her. Being a different species should make this impossible but hope and eagerness grew within me. I was content to be of use to her without such a thing, but I hissed out, "No," through my clenched teeth.

Even if it was futile to hope for more than what we already had, a primal part of me needed to fill her. I was born in the wild of the desert, a leader of my feral tribe, and with my seed heavy and aching, I could no longer resist with my mate squirming upon me.

My mate, I thought as I adjusted her for receiving me. The head of my cock warmed against her entrance, making me shudder as I felt the resistance of her tight seam. Her heel pulled forward, and I slowly stretched her to take my cock.

Control waned as I hissed at the pleasure of thrusting until my sack nestled against her. Her walls squeezed around me, and then I felt my body seize up. My muscles warmed, and I held my breath, feeling the way every inch of me tingled. I'd never felt anything like it. Others described to me what it was like to have a mate, and I hadn't thought I would experience it myself. It was like something untouchable was clicking into place, and even if I should unsheathe myself, this fullness would never leave me again. It seemed like such a ridiculous concept when described out loud, but made perfect sense in this moment.

But did she feel the same? Was this safe for her? Giving her my seed when she was under the influence of my mating hormones and covered in my oils seemed much too dubious and had me questioning my sanity.

"Treasure?"

A devious gleam entered her eyes after she unclasped herself from my neck, sending a jolt to my loins.

Then she said something that stilled my heart.

"You are mine."

I nodded, and all control was lost. All previous concerns exploded, and my tail secured her as I slammed deep inside her. In and out, I felt that tantalizing bundle of nerves at the entrance of her tight seam vibrate along my shaft as I moved. Great sun and stars. I'd never felt anything like her. That stimulation along my scales made my glands tighten and coil, pleasure surging through down to my bones, and deep into my blood.

My tail curved around her perfect ass that had thankfully filled out within the medpod since the first time I felt it when she was near starving. The thought made me grit my teeth with frustration that I wasn't there to prevent such a state of abuse. I was angry with myself for not finding her sooner, and I slammed into her harder, faster, reveling in the way she mewled and moaned with the pleasure that I was responsible for. Knowing I brought that dazed look to her bright glowing green eyes, and I was the reason her fingers dug into my back as she clung to me, was intoxicating.

I slipped my tail along the roundness of her ass, and between the valley between those plumped cheeks. My tincture oil lubricated my scales and made her skin slick as I put pressure at the divot of a tight hole that reminded me of the glands my species had to help heighten a female's pleasure. We'd plug their pleasure center with our tails to loosen the flap that would prevent our seed from reaching their eggs. Making them orgasm with these glands helped fill them with our seed. I'd never wanted to fill a hole so desperately as I did just then upon noticing it was there. My seed was so tight, and I knew I would release soon as I slapped against her, invigorated by her joyous sounds of growing pleasure. I could feel the way her muscles twitched the same way they did that first time she came on my tail. She was close to reaching her peak, and I wished to reach that with her.

My tail eased between her cheeks and pushed into that channel that squeezed upon my invasion, but as her little whimpers shortened and her heart rate increased, I captured her mouth and dove deeper, thrusting from both ends. I could feel my tail's pressure as I filled her from the front and groaned. My scales expanded inside her, sending me over the edge as my seed shot inside.

My treasure screamed as she clenched around me, and her muscles tensed up as she clung to my shoulders, her heels digging into my thighs. I kept rocking as my cum pumped and my scales expanded more to keep it from spilling. As I thrust again, I hissed instinctual objection to the loss of my seed dripping down my sack. It flexed again to fill her more, shooting more cum inside her. I moved one of my fingers, retracting my claw, to adjust under her thigh and scooped up my seed from between us and found myself pushing my finger back inside her, stretching her alongside my cock. I eased my finger in, and my other felt the delicious pulse of her clit. My tail twitched inside her ass, and she moaned, moving against me as her fangs scratched at my lips. I cared not that she took my blood inside her. In fact, it drove me wild with more need to see her shatter once more.

Rotating little circles on her clit, I loved the way her jaw trembled in her kisses as I worked my tail and my fingers, keeping my cock still to allow it the time it needed to empty my seed fully.

I whispered within her savage kisses, "You take me so well, Treasure."

She bit down on my lip with a growl. I chuckled with a joy I had never felt before this moment. My tongue licked at the blood she elicited from the act of need I recognized as the building orgasm working its way through her glowing body.

"That's right, take what you want, mate," I reveled in the way she pulsed around me.

"You," she said, while gripping my head and bringing me back to her lips. "You are mine."

On your lips, in your soul, I am yours until the stars take me, I thought, as the last of my seed made my body convulse and spasm with a groan of pleasure.

Blackness crept at the corners of my vision, and my tail lost feeling first as it slipped from her ass. A smile was plastered to my face, as I carefully guided my mate to the ground, and I knew she wasn't a trill, but I'd sleep now. I felt the tug of unconsciousness as my body naturally wished to make sure I remained inside my mate for as long as possible. It was typically a female's choice to wake a mated male or keep them unconscious and eat them for the nourishment of our spawn.

My fate was truly in her grasp, as the last thing I saw were her green eyes looking adorably content before I felt her curl into my hold to sleep with me.

Chapter Sixteen

Hazel

When I woke from the haze of a mating I would never forget for the rest of my cycles, a blanket was draped over us. And I yawned, cuddling deeper into Yueril's cozy hold.

"Yueril?" I asked when he still wasn't stirring from sleep. I'd have thought he was dead with how his heartbeat was not detectable, but that was normal for a trill, and I definitely could feel the throb of his cock fluttering inside me. His scales were still flexed and moved with every soft breath, barely noticeable from his mouth.

"I've never witnessed a trill mating before," Genbi said, startling me with a squeak.

"You're still here?"

"It is the command of the ship," he said, with a dismissive tone. "I do have preparations to attend to, and I found your mating noises soothing to listen to. I've never been so productive before," he explained with pride.

I crinkled my nose with the odd way he described my mating as a soundtrack for focused productivity. "Uh, right." This next part was going to be even more embarrassing to admit, but I've never been with anyone before, and I had no idea what was normal for post mating, especially with another species. I opened my mouth a few times to ask, but thankfully Genbi answered without me needing to voice anything further.

"I sent for one of the other trill on the ship to come up to the command to explain mating customs. He'll be along shortly. You've both been sleeping for longer than I'm personally comfortable with, and I'm just about finished up with what's needed to disembark back towards Delta-Fal. I've already done trades with Krelis to restock, and the time for distraction for your mate to sneak on to the planet during our departure is fast approaching."

Just then, the command door slid open and a trill, covered from head to toe in their usual robes, entered.

"Our ship is ready to depart, and the crew for the Krelis bindle stealth ship has been readied, waiting Commander Yueril," he stated before his eyes landed on the lump of tangled limbs that were his commander and myself. He cleared his throat, obviously uncomfortable with the sight.

A strange sound hissed from the trill as he exclaimed, "Great Goddess, I'll return later."

"No need," Genbi dismissed casually. "They've been like that for a while. I didn't call you up for a report on your preparations. I can see those from here." He motioned to the monitors. "You will tell me of your mating customs, and why your commander has not woken from his activities."

"He hasn't woken?" The trill asked with confusion. He lifted a brow ridge and scales from his head flexed and moved the hood of his robes back. "But you are not trill," he said with accusation towards me.

"What does that have to do with the mating?" Genbi redirected for me.

The trill cleared their throat to answer, "We do not go into forced hibernation unless severely injured, or we've released our seed into a mate for the first time. It's a custom for the female to kill an unwanted mate or wake them after to confirm they've accepted being marked. But," he scrambled after, "we do not release seed to pleasure our glands. That is not possible. He must be injured..."

"He isn't," Genbi replied with ease.

I flushed at the implications and the memory of how full Yueril filled me with his cum. Even now, I felt the moisture drip from my mating loh, still my seam was warm and unsealed after mating. My eyes widened at my stupidity. I had no idea that my mating loh wouldn't close, and I fell asleep with his cock nestled inside of me with no thought about if he would get stuck after we finished.

"How do we wake him?" I asked shyly, hiding behind Yueril's wide shoulders.

"Through a mate mark," the trill sighed out with exasperation, like that would be impossible. I nuzzled into Yueril's neck and felt my fangs extend as I approached where I bit him. With gentle care, I sunk my fangs in, and Yueril twitched. I smiled into his scales and suckled. A low moan escaped my throat as his hips jolted and his cock hardened inside of me.

I looked up from where I bit my mate and watched with a strange satisfaction as the trill stared. He watched in horror, and undeniable lust. A jealousy clouded his features that I recognized from when I held that same gaze looking on at my clan mating at the hot spring without me. My moan grew louder as his claws dug into my ass, and he woke to pumping his thick cock within my eager mating loh.

That's right, my love, fill me again, I thought with glee and uncaring about our audience.

"My cock is yours, Treasure, and I'll fill that needy loh until it can't hold more of me, and I must push it back up to remind you where I belong," he groaned into my ear.

He had no idea we had an audience, and I wasn't going to spoil the mood by reminding him until he did exactly what he promised. The trill seemed to be a bit skittish about public displays, but he used his tail to help flip me to my back as he leaned over me.

His dark eyes watched me with ferocity, then his eyes lifted to stare down the trill with a grin on his face as he pumped inside of me and hissed, "Mine."

I guided his attention back to me and pulled his head down to kiss me. "Yours," I whispered back, as tears prickled my eyes with joy that he was awake and unharmed.

His hands trailed over my loh and the sound of his hips slapping into me was music to my ears as I embraced the sensations of how deeply he filled me, beyond the sensitive spot at the back of my mating loh, but ingrained in my very flesh and blood.

My skin was on fire, and I glowed so brightly as my muscles coiled and anticipated release.

"Louder," he demanded.

"Yours!" I screamed as his cock thrust inside of me again, faster, deeper. I could feel the way my limbs were losing control, and I dug my hands into my hair and arched into the pleasure. My hands flew out of my strands to grab for something more substantial. One hand gripped my breast and pinched my nipple, squeezing and rubbing to ease the ache inside of me that I knew would only come from feeling him finish, and the sensation of overflowing with his seed. My remaining hand gripped his hip to feel each slap of our bodies melding together.

"I need..." I panted, trying to tell him that I needed him to cum inside me. "Please," I begged. The sensations were overwhelming and my release was so close.

He leaned over me, and his hand slipped over my curves to around my ass. I blushed, remembering how his tail heightened every touch when it pushed inside. His fingers were thicker than my species, and I wanted to know how it would feel to have him enter me there with his finger instead of his tail, but his finger passed over my hole and slipped to my loh, between my thighs and swirled in the cum that thickened there from the last time we mated. He moved the viscous liquid up and dragged his finger along the seam of my ass, to push within. I wiggled and willed myself to open as his cock slammed down and pushed his finger deeper.

He whispered with a possessiveness, "You will open for me, mate, and I will fill every part of you with my seed, with my venom, and my soul."

Then I felt the pressure of his cock pulsing his seed within me, his scales expanded, and I never felt so full and satisfied. I screamed, as my limbs stopped working and waves of heady ecstasy took over. I couldn't move as I arched into the way his cum jetted and his scales touched every bundle of sensitive nerves, leaving me trembling as he held me against him.

This time we did not sleep, but he kissed the top of my head, and I could feel the way he smiled into my hair. It was a different kind of fullness that had my heart aching.

The trill cleared his throat. He apparently was stunned in place, unable to stop himself from watching my mate claim my body. And it was his, I thought with a wry smile.

Yueril's tail wrapped around me to help hold us together as he stood and faced our company, with me still attached.

The trill bowed their head to their commander, averting their eyes.

"My mate has accepted my mark," he said joyfully to his crewmate, unashamed.

"As the stars shine from the future, and we bask in their past, may your mating be fruitful," the trill did a strange gesture with their pinky finger, which was their smallest finger, though still not much smaller than their main finger, or their thumb, at their forehead and then added, "In many we rise."

"In many we rise, Hedenpawl," Yueril said happily. The other trill gaped at him. I assumed it was because Yueril had used his name, which was a rarity for a trill to do. "Perhaps the impossible is not so impossible after all. Let's do the same and go fetch my second for the wonderful news. Belder has a promise to keep. She swore that if I were to mate, that she would be so shocked that she would personally bless my union and even teach me how she gets the synthesizer to make the meat taste less like reconstituted gum and more like chummed pie."

"I doubt she'll keep that promise. That is a prized secret of hers," the trill, Hedenpawl, joked. At least, I thought it was humor, since it was difficult to tell with the trill it seemed.

I smiled up at the unabashed, dangerous gleam of my mate. He was not worried about scaring anyone with showing off his sharp teeth anymore. He held me against him with such devotion and pride that I warmed at the sight.

Chapter
Seventeen
Hazel

W e parted ways with the Birds of Zorn, though I knew the demise of their previous lord would not stop the gray deeds of their nefarious trade, but I hoped that with new leadership, whoever that would be, there would be a change for the better. Belder, it seemed, didn't need our help in the way we had previously anticipated. She was staying with them of her own choice and went willingly to Krelis because of an outbreak of what they called the molt fever.

Both Yueril and myself knew better. Many krelins were dying and the fever had nothing to do with molting, or anything natural. We made the decision to use our last reserve of the Ganpan-Fal to save the planet and kept some samples to research a way of making the nanobots replicate more efficiently before the Solusgors could have a chance to try again in the future.

I stood in the lab, looking out at the stars beyond Estreldez, on the farthest moon, Bina. Behind me the doors opened with a wheeze, and a warmth of power made my loh react with a glow of their own. I knew without turning that the Almder entered the room, and I doubted she would have come herself, yet here she was.

Taking a deep breath, I hardened myself to face her and stilled. She was more stunning than I could have imagined. I'd never seen her outside of the sculptures depicted of her. They didn't do her justice. Her hair was long and braided like a netting across her white strands. Her loh were colorless and bright like clear flawless crystals. Her back loh extended out from her shoulders like lethal wings, putting my own loh to shame. She was like a moon goddess, and I could feel my knees grow weak, like I should kneel before her. I held strong, refusing to bend to her powerful presence. She had much to answer for.

Yueril gave me the space to handle this on my own, though, he was just in the other room if I had need of him. Just the knowledge that I could rely on him, if necessary, gave me the strength to do this. To face her.

She touched her lithe, long fingers to her crown where a green loh was placed. The strong, stern look I was expecting from the leader of Estreldez crumbled as tears welled in her icy blue eyes. Her lip trembled.

She plucked the small loh from the crown and pointed to my birthmark just below my collarbone. "May I?" she asked carefully.

I wasn't sure what she was doing, but I nodded, unable to refuse her. She placed the small loh in the deep green dark spot my mom said was where I lost a loh during my spawning. The Almder sniffled and choked up as she saw how the loh fit the shape of my mark.

She picked up my limp hand and placed the loh in my palm, wrapping my fingers around it. Guiding it, along with her hand covering my fist back to the mark.

"I took this loh, above where your heart beat, thinking it was the closest I'd ever get before you returned to the great rock. They told me you did not survive." She sucked in a quivering breath.

All thoughts of how I would handle this meeting vanished. If she did not know that I was living near the mountain, or even that I was alive...

My heart crumbled and bled for her, for us, for the time we've lost, but then Ordin's words returned to me, that she had banished her own mate, and stripped him of his mating loh.

"Is it true?" I forced out, ruining the moment, and taking a step away from her for more clarity of thought beyond the emotions roaring through me.

She blinked away her tears and stared at me with a soft bewilderment at my question and the way I retreated from her.

"They told me you died," she said, appearing stricken that I would not believe her, but that wasn't what I meant.

"Ordin," I tried to jog her memory, and her lips pursed in displeasure.

"If it was up to him, you would not exist at all," she snipped, and the aura of authority and power of being a leader that had to make a tough decision sharpened her features.

"You sent him away to become a monster," I forced the issue.

"I did what I had to do," she dismissed, a hard line to her mouth as she wiped at her tears with the heel of her hand. "I'd lost many offspring and found out that it was because of him that they returned to the rock instead of standing beside the both of us today. I banished him, took what was mine, and I'd do it again today if given the choice."

I didn't understand and she could see the confusion in my eyes and her eyes softened like she had raised me my whole life. "He did not tell you that he was the reason the offspring died? Unable to accept his responsibility even to this rising." She chided.

"He's dead," I couldn't help myself but to add.

She gave a curt nod of acceptance and continued, "I couldn't bring myself to do the deed, but it is what he deserved for murdering our offspring. Every time he found me swollen with life, he went to the mountains and plucked the poisoned root of arnut to add to my meals so I would bleed the offspring from my body before it could thrive."

My jaw slackened at the idea that someone would do such a thing, but Ordin spoke of how he believed the Almder was killing herself to have another offspring. Perhaps he thought he would save her by making sure she didn't conceive? I shook my head as another horrifying realization struck.

I didn't wish to say it out loud, but living on my own for so long, I wasn't able to censor my thoughts as I processed them, "What if, he never poisoned her food... but someone else did, or even an accidental contamination of the food supply that kept making her ill, also leading to the miscarriage of offspring... Perhaps, no one was to blame, or someone else entirely? How does she know it was him? He was so certain that the offspring was what was killing her..."

"Have you been able to have any other offspring?" I finally asked her, louder this time, as it was now my intention to be heard.

She shook her head in the negative, appearing appalled by the idea that someone may still be poisoning her, or there really was a contamination that could be affecting more than herself and potential declines in offspring from others in the clan.

"I'll have my brightest investigate further, if you feel I've mis-judged Ordin," she said with a sad smile, but the way she shook her head told me she didn't believe it was an issue, and even if it was, she had no regrets for what she'd done to her mate. The words of Vareo lingered in my mind that all leaders are capable of dark things. "As my only living heir, you will stay and learn what you must to lead our clan," she added, like she was simply discussing what kind of minerals to eat for dinner.

"I'd like to learn from your scientists here, on Bina, on how to help with the potential contamination, and medical technology, such as programming nanobots," I blurted out before she could dismiss me.

"Of course, My Jewel, anything you desire," she easily agreed.

"I'm mated," I added.

"Yes," she said with a smile. "It is blessed news should your union bring offspring to the clan. And I've already agreed to your mate's terms that your identity remains secret until we are certain no one will harm you again. It was his only stipulation for allowing you to stay with me. Of course, practically, I am granting him a stay as your mate, but he must remain on Bina, aside from approved visitations within the clan. His species would not do well on the mainland; the moon's rays would not suit him when amplified by tarnpul. I won't have my son-in-law shrivel up before giving me offspring to dote over."

I blushed at the idea and absently placed my hands over my stomach with yearning.

Before I realized it, Yueril was entering the room and kissing my forehead. I didn't know how long I had stood there day-dreaming of what kind of offspring we'd have together. Would they be more like Yueril, with scales and a tail? Or would they be more like me with bright loh, and five fingers? My eyes grew wide... would they be bald with scales? I shook my head. The idea of not having any hair at all was odd to me, but Yueril was more than fine without a single hair on his body. And what a body it was, I thought as he scooped me into his arms.

"What thoughts are stirring in that head of yours?" he asked.

I didn't want to worry him with thoughts of offspring we may never have, so I frowned, unsure what to say before I set-tled on avoiding the question all together. "Are you sure you're alright with your crew leaving without you?"

"Belder is a fine commander. They will survive without me," he assured and then placed his large hand over mine, which was somehow still resting on my stomach. "Our future will survive too."

I smiled at that. It was the best way to think about things. I had a future now, with him, and a very important mission to figure out the next steps with the nanotechnology that saved our lives for now, but for how long? Whatever happens, we'd face it together. Lifting his hand in mine to my lips, I whispered, "The fate of the stars are here. Small stars fade with the eye. Large stars destroy the sky. We break under pressure and electrify. Our future will survive."

Chapter
Eighteen
Yueril

"You need to take a break," Hazel insisted. Her voice echoed in my implant, a sign that the technology was degrading over the years of exposure to the moon's radiation. It made sense why the estrelds didn't use the technology themselves and kept their planet isolated. Their queen, whom they called Almder, has maintained her desire to avoid diplomats that have found their way out to the far reaches of the galaxy.

"It's almost ready. The krelins have already took trade ships full of Ordin without supplying the hewve lard, nectar, or rekol rock. They are changing trade demands, and your Almder may not be planning for an invasion, but one will come. They act like this planet is already theirs."

My breathing hissed out in more of a wheeze as I made sure another satellite was finished for launch around the moon. I assured myself it had nothing to do with my frustrations at the Almder's lack of action. The net circuit was almost completed.

"She's right, I can finish this up," the young male named Loric said with a stoic demeanor. He was a serious sort of youngling but had advised with the Almder on my behalf to make this defense system a priority. "Almder told me that your room was designed to repel the moon's radiation. You'll shrivel up into a worm if you stay out here much longer."

"That is an exaggeration," I assured him.

"You still promise that you won't return to the great rock if you train me in combat?" Loric lifted a brow ridge at me as I scratched at my dry scalp scales.

"The only rock you're returning to is the one where you remind our offspring that she is not to moon bathe on the tarnpul anymore. She is as stubborn as you are," my treasure complained, though I could hear the way her tone changed like her mouth was smiling as she said it. Hazel's green skin had been fading over the years, starting where the loh on her feet were removed, turning pink. Less and less radiation was being converted by her delicate loh jewels, which made me wish to work faster to protect her. As strong as she was, she would not be able to fight as she used to. Another surge like she gave her father could be her last.

"Yes, the tarnpul is dangerous when not treated properly," I agreed. "I'll remind her that tarnpul can drain radiation as quickly as it gives it if she isn't careful." I returned my attention to the blue jeweled estreld, only half my size, yet so grown up. "You can train with Faith. You two are the same cycles, and perhaps you can remind her of the dangers of untreated tarnpul."

"She made my whole arm go numb last time," Loric complained.

"All the more reason to train. It's best to avoid the tincture oil near her scales, and it'll better prepare you for defending yourself against krelin musk."

"How am I supposed to win if I can't touch her?"

"A krelin's musk is only useful in close proximity. They use their wings to blow it into your face before it can dilute itself within the air's radiation. They must be close, just like you must touch the oil for it to numb you. You're still young, but there is no shame in using tools to even a duel."

I handed him the tarnpul pole I carried around, it was treated to repel radiation, and the boy flinched as he grasped it, but he didn't drop it. He nodded and pressed the button on its center to collapse it to a smaller stick the size of my leg, larger than his own small frame. It would grow with him.

He still seemed confused by the gesture, and I smiled at how he still maintained his composure. He'd be a fine warrior one day. "If it repels the radiation around it, then it can be swung to deflect a krelin's musk. It also makes sure that when you are training, you are not relying on your loh's radiation, but on your own strength. It gives you an advantage that you can train to defeat someone without your loh, while others will struggle to do something they have not yet trained for."

"Are you trying to kill Almder's favorite youngling?" Hazel interrupted my guidance for the youngling from my implant, that had yet to break the communication connection.

"He won't die from holding tarnpul, and he can train to hold the pole and stop it from interfering with his loh, just as our daughter should do before she goes moon bathing again."

"Remind him that he shouldn't carry it with him all the time. Only for training. He still needs the moon's rays to be healthy and grow strong, and if you've given him your pole then it would repel too much of the radiation from reaching his loh. I'll go to the market to buy another one for you. Ezra won't be pleased that you've given it away. It was a gift, you know."

"Now, it is still a gift," I dismissed her worries. We both knew that living on Estreldez was difficult for my species, and like my time in the deserts of Trillume, I was seen as a savage by much of the clan that knew of my existence.

"Almder says that the net you're building could damage our moon's ability to fuel our planet's rocks with nutrients," Loric said while flipping the condensed pole up in the air and failing to catch it when it returned to the ground. He frowned and tried again.

"To create something is an act of destroying what it was before. Even this tarnpul we've used to build these satellites, will never be the same. For you to live, there are rocks and plants that are ground up into mulch. If the krelins attack, then it is a price your planet will pay to survive."

"They will," Loric grunted about the krelins, as he thrust the pole forward like it was a sword.

"They already have," I corrected him. The ships that sent trade between our planets were no longer under Estreldez control. Our moon's filled up the ships for less and less in return each time they arrived. The trade routes were turning more into a tribute to keep them from invading than a real source of benefit for the planet and the clan.

When I arrived back to the dwelling on Bina's outpost, I found my treasure scrolling through code on her screens. And then a voice filled the room from the speakers, "The samples you gave me have been processed. You were right, the water supply from the mountain is clean, but the waterfall has arnut root growing on the rock wall behind it. Half of our water supply comes from there."

"Even so," Hazel said with a shake of her head, "Arnut root must be crushed to activate, and it would be in the rock wall itself. It would've had to fall from the wall, exposing the roots to the water, and not in high concentration. It doesn't add up."

"Yes, the trace amounts found at the waterfall shouldn't have been enough to cause the miscarriages. We have a team carefully removing the arnut from the wall without further contaminating the water. We'll dig up some of the tunnels to do some more tests between the falls and the clan."

"I am not the only one in need of a break," I whispered into her ear as she jolted a bit from her chair at my quiet approach.

"Great moons!" she yelped.

"Hazel?" the scientist from the labs questioned with concern.

"I'm fine," she huffed out. "Take care of my sister."

"The Almder's pregnancy is progressing nicely. It's the last of your father's seed and if it weren't for you, the princess may never have been given a chance. You know the Almder asks about you often..."

My mate sighed and wrapped her hand behind my neck to pull me against her. Her head nuzzled into my neck for strength. This was hard on her to keep her distance, but our daughter wasn't the only stubborn one on this moon.

"It isn't about us anymore, is it?" she finally said, the message not for me, but for her mother.

"Tell the Almder that the net is functional as it is but still has some blind spots to fix. There is a risk of using it too soon and a link failing. A link failure could result in pulling too much radiation too fast from the planet's surface. It is better to allow the radiation net to slowly fuel itself without directly drawing from the moons or the planet."

"You can tell her yourself," they replied.

"I don't plan on using it at all, my son," the Almder spoke from the speaker, having been on the call, it seemed, the whole time.

"You will have need of it," I said with measured words to keep my temper in check. Why allow me to build it if she won't use it to defend her planet?

"It is nothing more than a warning. A show to keep the krelin from overstepping again. My hope is that they see it and decide to waste their efforts in trying to dismantle covertly, while we continue to repair it as quickly as they decide to push their limits. This game will keep them busy enough while we train our clan to defend itself. Loric is one of our most promising offspring. I'll have a team assigned to monitoring the moon net, and a lab built on our largest moon to keep up with maintenance."

"A show is only as powerful as its performance. A sign won't tell the krelins anything," I muttered through gritted teeth. I would have to discuss our options to leave Estreldez if the Almder wasn't willing to defend my mate and my lifeborn. My daughter, Faith, would see war if the net went unused.

Hazel's fingers massaged through my scales, and I felt the heat in my veins quickly shift from agitation to something that required this communication to end immediately for more enjoyable endeavors.

"There is great risk in using the net," Hazel reasoned, her voice soothing despite my disagreement of how to protect this planet. "At least, the risk is greater when it hasn't had enough time to safely accumulate a radiation field."

"According to my calculations, it's possible a net failure could result in draining radiation from the planet's surface instead of the moons," the scientist added.

"Which is why, if the net must be used at all, every estreld would have to take refuge beneath a Glorbin Flower enforced bunker to be sure that they wouldn't be drained themselves," Hazel continued, "Lucky for us all, the palace has many glorbin decorated rooms, and an underground tarnpul oasis big enough for the whole clan. You should consider doing emergency drills for everyone to know where to go."

"That shouldn't be a worry when the net is complete," I countered, ending on a groan as Hazel's other hand reached behind to rub at my mating glands.

"Then complete the net, and perhaps the krelins will not confiscate the satellites too quickly to erode the safety of using it all together," the Almder replied, though I could hear the sarcasm in her voice. She was certain that the net would always be too risky to use. She accommodated the building of the net for Hazel and liked to see the drive of the youngling Loric taking initiative, but she had no intention of using it. Intention or not, having the option as a last resort was better than having no resort at all when the krelins came for them. And they would.

My second, Belder, sent messages through the trade ships. The human she was helping there was deteriorating, and she feared that his death would break the queen's mind on believing Estreldez was already hers by control of our trade. There wouldn't be much time. If my second was correct, then when that human died... so too would this fragile truce. Control of the trade wouldn't be enough.

"Yueril is certain that with the current set up that it could safely disarm a ship without demanding too much from the net. The risk is in trying to harness the radiation not already stored in the satellites," Hazel explained.

What she wasn't saying was that if my information about the Krelis Queen was accurate then there wouldn't be enough time to use the radiation net safely, nor enough time to train the clan on how to defend itself. The estrelds weren't warriors, and without using the satellites... this planet would be overrun by the krelins.

"I will not say this again," the Almder said with a serious tone that did not allow for distraction or disagreement, "The palace is not the only clan on Estreldez. Many smaller clans live across the lands, the deserts, and mountains. We have farmers who train hergslats and live with the herds. We have many who choose to live as our ancestors have without the comforts of the palace and the city, out in the open, with no emergency bunkers to hide in, nor a way of knowing that they should be hiding at all. To use this net, would mean to commit those estrelds to death in favor of saving approximately twenty percent of Estreldez in the case of link failure."

After a static pause she added, "Would you sacrifice yourself, your mate, your offspring for the chance that an untested radiation net saves a small twenty percent of the planet from what? Being held prisoner to giving tributes to the krelins? Giving them the title of sovereign over the clans that would most likely be alive to rebel in the future? Do you not think that we could send a distress signal to the trill to keep more than such a small number? I should not have to say this much. What you ask for is too much. The net will always be a threat and nothing more. I will not speak on it again."

The communication ended, and silence filled the room as I stared at the wall, stunned by the Almder's resolve.

Only Hazel's voice pulled me from my thoughts on how she gave the krelins too much credit for how they would rule over this planet if given the chance.

"She doesn't want to understand what they would do with most of us. If they harvest our loh for trade exports... becoming nothing more than commodities for them to sell. It would be a horribly way to die."

My treasure had survived what the krelins had done to her, but not without a bit of luck on her side. Many estrelds were not so lucky. It wasn't until we returned to Estreldez that she confessed that she wasn't the only one taken when she was grabbed. At the very same waterfall she spoke of earlier, another female was taken. She thinks often of how an estreld she never truly knew was still gone, and likely dead from being harvested like The Zorn had wanted to do to her. Her experience was one of many the Almder refused to acknowledge.

There was no telling how many estrelds were taken during each trade visit, and none of them were being reported to the palace that we knew of. Hazel stood from her chair and cupped my chin to face her instead of the wall, lost in my absent thoughts of how many I was unable to save. The new radiation net should stop unsanctioned landings on the main planet without notifying us of a disturbance in the links.

It was most likely the only reason the Almder allowed us to build it, and the only acknowledgement we'd ever receive about what was happening to Estreldez outside of the city and the largest clan on the planet.

"Faith will not be taken by the krelins," Hazel promised like she was threatening the goddess should she fail to protect our daughter. She was safely with Ezra on the main planet, deep within the desert, and we would know if a spaceship passed through the net to try to land near there. Ezra was the lead researcher in the clan and an old friend of the woman who took care of Hazel, the estreld she grew up knowing as her mom.

"She has something you didn't," I assured my mate. "She has us, and she will not be sheltered in ignorance of what she is capable of." Faith was born with her mother's attributes of many beautiful loh jewels in a light pinkish hue, and yellow eyes like my own. Her skin is scaled around her loh, and covering sensitive areas to protect her vital organs, but they are the same coloring as her skin, allowing her to blend well with other estrelds. I was saddened to see she didn't inherit a tail, but it was common for estreld traits to be dominated by the mother's attributes. The offspring took on traits more like their mother than their male counterparts. It was pleasing enough to see that Faith had spikes in her hair, letting me know that one day she could defend herself as my ancestors had.

Faith would know how to use her loh in defense, her tincture oils to give her an advantage, and learn to fight as if she had no advantages at all.

"It's our job to make sure she never has to test those capabilities beyond her training," Hazel said with a heavy sigh. "The clan believes training warriors is because the Almder wishes to open up our mating ceremonies to offworlders in the future, that opening up our trade beyond Krelis will protect us from their invasion. None of them realize how close we are to war."

"I'll be ready!" Faith said from the doorway, but what I saw immediately was her lovely green skin marred from her fingers up to her shoulder. I hissed in distress as I made my way to our injured lifeborn.

"What has happened to you," I gritted out while examining for cracks in her loh jewels, she had so few of them, that a single damaged loh could be life-threatening.

"Oh, that happened when I was next to the tarnpul," she said dismissively, like it was nothing.

"What did we say about moon bathing on untreated tarnpul!" Hazel was already beside me struggling between anger and concern.

Faith scoffed. "It's nothing, watch," she said while she concentrated her loh and the black faded from her skin and scales. Until all that was left were a few trace amounts at the fingertips that colored her nails black.

My second eyelid slid over to check on the glow of her radiation, and nothing seemed out of the ordinary about the beautiful heat pulsing from her like a star. Then she grabbed my claws and concentrated once more. Her skin turned green.

"Your loh are controlling the manner in which the moon's rays are reflecting from your skin..." Hazel said in awe.

"Pretty neat, right?" Faith said with excitement. "It's easier to do around the tarnpul, that's why I've been moon bathing there so often. I almost got my whole torso to be black!"

I paled at the image of my lifeborn bathing with no robes to notice if her whole torso had changed or not. I cleared my throat. "You are wearing your robes?"

She rolled her eyes at me. "Dad," Faith groaned.

"I just don't want anyone spying on you. You are not old enough for mating," I reasoned with her.

"It is important to wear your robes," Hazel agreed, though for different reasons. "I don't want anyone making fun of you for having less loh than them. I've heard rumors of younglings being bullied for the number of loh they have, and you have more scales than loh."

"They are beautiful," I added quickly. The advice was sound, but what estrelds valued in mates wasn't exclusive to loh prominence, as my own treasure could attest. I had none myself. Scales were a blessing.

With a kick of dust at her boots, Faith pouted, "No one is looking, anyway. You both stay on Bina, more than at the palace, or Elder Ezra's place. Almder says that I can't stay with Elder Ezra for a few cycles because the krelins are sending warriors to discuss trade agreements."

"That's why you're back early," Hazel said with a shake of her head, since we were just on a communication with Almder and not a word was said about our lifeborn returning, nor the incoming krelins."

Chapter Nineteen

Hazel

"M om?"

"Mmhmm..." I mumbled, distracted with comparing the skin samples to make sure she was safe.

"Mom," she repeated with annoyance.

"Yes, hmm?" I pried myself from the images I was zoomed in on. It couldn't be possible, could it?

"Dad's going to the mines again instead of waiting for the next link stuff to come in. He's making Loric babysit me," she whined.

"That hasn't upset you before," I dismissed her concern over Loric watching her. She shouldn't be testing her loh's abilities without someone to monitor for trouble. The krelins could come at any time, it wasn't safe.

She huffed. "He's wearing a full mask and can't even hear most of what I'm saying without connecting with an earpiece."

I smiled knowing why she was upset now. It was typical to find Loric unconscious when Faith decided she was done being watched. "You're not planning on trying to spray him with your tincture oil again, are you?"

She's become more resourceful and spent a whole week collecting her sweat and oils into a canister that she used to spray in concentration, paralyzing Loric's body on multiple occasions since Yueril found out the krelins would be here soon. Faith has been on strict probation to remain within the protection of the Bina moon outpost, especially when a shuttle is available. Yueril worries that she will sneak aboard to get back to the main clan while it's not safe for her.

"No," Faith said the word with a guilty elongation as if extending the short answer would somehow excuse her for planning to harm Loric again.

"Faith," I exhaled in exhaustion at having to repeat my warnings, "How many times must I tell you that you could really hurt Loric one of these times if he inhales the tincture oils. What if you paralyze his lungs and he is unable to breathe? Your oils are meant to numb live meat for eating, not escaping your father's request for you to be protected."

She gives me a disgusted look, but the sharp front teeth confirm her nature to need more than rocks to survive like her father.

"Ugh, you know I spray at his feet first. The oil is too heavy to lift up in the air. Dad said I should spray to disable first."

"Of course he did," I said with a groan. Turning my head back to the images of her skin cells to hide the smile lifting at the corners of my mouth at knowing Yueril still tried to give Faith the tools to learn how to escape even his own protection detail of sending the boy Loric to watch her.

"Come here, I need to show you something," I changed the subject.

"Is that my skin?" she asked.

"Some of them," I confirmed. "Do you see the difference?"

"Not really," she exhaled with defeat.

"It's subtle," I assured her that it would be normal to overlook if no one is trying to see something different. "It's easy to think they are all the same, and there were other pressing issues to study. See here," I pointed to the zoomed in image, "This is your loh, and this one is one of your scales, and this one," I got more excited, "and this one is your skin!" I grabbed her by the shoulders and turned her to look at another set of images. "This is my skin, my loh, and another randomly selected skin and loh sample. Do you see it?"

I didn't wait for her to answer before I burst out, "Your skin and scales activate the same as loh. Your whole body absorbs the moon's rays, even your hair! We were worried that you wouldn't get enough radiation because your larger loh were so few, but you're able to absorb radiation better than anyone I've ever seen. And because of your scales, you're able to mask your radiation, and not dry out your oils because your scales ARE no different than loh."

By now, I'm holding her shoulders in front of me and staring her down with the largest grin on my face. She was safe. Her life wasn't at risk because of her scales. She was safer because of them. Mating with a trill gave her strength. Strength that would defend my Faith from the krelins, and give us insight that our skin is no different than our loh.

"All of our skin is simply millions of smaller loh that haven't been activated like yours have. If we can figure out what activated yours, then the whole clan will be safer."

"Seems like you've made a discovery that could be a problem for my commander," a young male voice spoke from the entry way.

"Faith... behind me," I said while putting myself between her and the krelin that had made its way inside my home. It wasn't the time to ask her if she forgot to lock the doors behind her when she entered from the training grounds. Krelins could fly into open areas like the courtyard, but they shouldn't have been able to land without the links being notified of interference in the atmosphere.

"Where is Loric?" I whispered over my shoulder.

"I'm sorry. I didn't mean to..." she whimpered. "I didn't think..."

"Is Loric the halfling I found crawling on the ground?" The krelin asked with a smirk. "He didn't put up much of a fight after I removed his mask."

"What have you done to him?" Faith screamed at him while pushing past me to charge the krelin.

"Faith!" I scrambled after her. She's never faced a krelin before.

Her hand was out with the canister of her tincture oil ready to spray at the krelin's face. His wings snapped out from behind him, a gust of wind defending from the spray reaching his face, but I watched as he grabbed her wrist. The canister dropped to the floor with a clank. Faith grunted as pulled the krelin in closer to her, like her father taught her. I cursed Yueril for teaching her to go towards danger. He'd say the enemy never expects someone to lean into an attack, and her scales and oils were designed for close combat. The krelin was too confident in his own abilities to wear much protection, and I watched as my own flesh and blood rubbed her skin against him to paralyze him.

There was a look of shock on the krelin's face, and a surge of hope filled me as I launched myself at him to help my daughter. His arms wrapped around her, and she yelped.

"Let go of me, you-- you--" she couldn't think of what to call him, as if her colorful vocabulary was too shocked to work after seeing the krelin's hold wasn't loosening.

I charged up my loh on my hands to burn him, my grip extended to rip through his wings if I had to. A strange musty scent filled my nose and itched down my throat. Fuck, I thought as I felt my own limbs grow weary. I grabbed onto his arm and put all my radiation into burning his flesh to release my Faith, my life, my very essence that he wrapped up in those lethal arms.

Flashes of my own abduction clogged up my throat, silencing my screams in my mind. This was not happening again, I pleaded to the goddess that this would not be my daughter's fate. Not again. Not after everything we've done to try to protect her.

My eyes grew heavy. I struggled to keep them open, but I felt the pressure of my nails digging into his arm, and then I reached up to claw at his face before my legs wobbled and fell beneath me. My own body betraying me just like at the waterfall.

"No," I whimpered barely above a whisper.

I watched from the floor as my daughter struggled in his hold.

"How are you still moving?" he grunted against her.

"I could ask you the same thing, you sick fuck!" Faith went limp, but I saw the way she pleaded with a look at me before she tensed up and pushed upward to knock him off balance. But krelins were harder to knock down with their wings supporting them, he simply lifted off the ground and floated with a push of his wingspan.

I was equally confused. Faith was still moving, the krelin musk not affecting her, and her tincture oils were not subduing him.

My worst fear was playing out before my eyes with nothing I could do.

"Are you playing with the estrelds, Li-aq?" Another male voice came from behind them.

"No, Commander," Li-aq he said still struggling to hold my daughter. "Why didn't my musk work like yours did on the other one?"

"You're still young," the commander said with sympathy. "It's possible your musk isn't fully developed, or..." he said ominously then tsked.

"What? Or what?" Li-aq panicked.

"Or this little estreld is a potential mate, but that would be very dangerous for the queen to even think about. She's just as likely to dispose of you as she is to let any of these estrelds get away with harboring the trill responsible for murdering her mate."

Murdering her mate?

That was news to me.

"The Almder hasn't murdered anyone, you psycho!" Faith hissed, and I heard the krelin holding her scream.

"The demon has sharp teeth!"

"Yes, estrelds do have retractable fangs used for drinking blood for the minerals when they are still young and unable to crush a sufficient number of rocks. This one is still not fully grown it seems," the commander said with a calm dismissiveness. "If you are unable to handle the youth, then perhaps I was hasty in bringing you on this important mission."

"Argh, no... I can handle it," he grunted before my eyes widened in distress. His mouth clamped down on my daughter's neck and she gasped before collapsing in his arms.

"We're here for the trill, kill these ones and meet me at the shuttle. We are on a time constraint. The shuttles are our only way to enter the main planet without being detected by their new radiation net."

The commander left, and my limbs remained too heavy to move. I'd pass out soon, because I was too late in activating my loh to burn off the musk. The other krelin had blood dripping down his face from where I scratched him down his eye, and he hissed as he shifted my daughter's weight from where I dug my other claws into his arm. It wasn't enough. I didn't disable him in time.

I failed, I thought with a growing ache in my chest.

He clucked from the back of his throat, and crouched down, gently placing my daughter next to me. "I should kill you," he whispered while tucking her hair behind her ear.

My own throat wouldn't answer my call to scream.

"You'll die with me," Faith choked out.

"Perhaps," he said with a wince while licking the blood dripping from his cheek where my nails had dug in. "But if we both live through this, I will find you again. I'll become a commander, and you'll carry a future queen of Krelis." His throat clucked, vibrating off the walls like a promise. "Try not to die, mate."

No, my mind screamed.

The young krelin left us, and my daughter's arms shook as she lifted her weight to check on me.

"Mom," she stroked my hair back, and sighed when she saw my eyes still open. "Guess the commander scum was right about his musk not being strong enough yet. Don't worry, I bit him. He won't survive the venom."

I whimpered.

I couldn't tell her that him biting her back changed everything. I still had her father's mark on my inner elbow. He had bonded me to make sure that I didn't die from his poison. I could only hope that they weren't mates, and the commander was wrong. Because if they were, then she marked him as hers and neither of them would be able to bond with someone else.

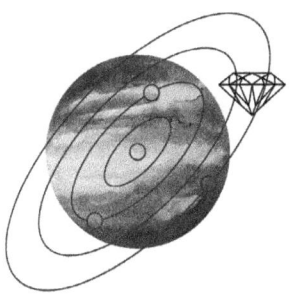

Chapter Twenty
Yueril

The buzz of wings alerted me before I saw them. How did they get past the moon's security? I slowed my heartrate to blend in with the sounds of the shuttle gearing up to leave. They wouldn't be able to track my heat or discern the sound of my breath from the buzz of their own wings. It was a white noise of their flight, and if they had wanted to sneak up on me, they wouldn't have used their wings at all. They even communicated with one another, the clucking of their throats echoed off the metal.

I'd have to remember to tell Hazel the shuttles should shut their doors closer to launch, but I knew she would tell me that safety goes both ways. Closing the doors could also be dangerous in trapping someone on a ship that hasn't passed all the system checks. She'd say the security of the docking station should be priority over the doors of the shuttle. I smiled, of course she was right. I'd focus on resecuring the dock after I killed the krelins daring to steal a shuttle.

I flattened myself against the wall, my tail at ready to stab whoever entered.

"Stay back, spawn," a deep voice echoed. "The trill will know we are here. We are not trying to hide from him, but your wounds leave you vulnerable to trill poison." A pause before he continued, "That's right, I have no fear of being poisoned by you. I'm wearing a trill robe made specifically to protect against being sprayed by you. And yes, you could kill the youngling, but he knows as well as I do that not every warrior survives a mission. He will die gladly, though I will be disappointed that I spent so much time training a warrior that couldn't survive his first mission."

Trill robes were designed to keep our poisons inside our robes, protecting those around us if our instincts triggered from being caught off guard. It would protect a wearer from another's poison, though that wasn't the original intent. Every trill protects their robes from getting into the wrong hands.

"It wasn't difficult to get one," he continued to gloat. "You see, we happen to have a trill on krelis who has no need for it anymore."

Belder... I felt my control faulter and a hiss escaped through my teeth.

If they killed Belder, this would be their end. My second in command was a kind heart who stayed behind on Krelis to help a human who was suffering there, and I wouldn't have been surprised to find her sympathizing with the krelins that thought they were keeping her against her will. She could have left any time she wished, but her big heart was likely the reason why they were able to kill her.

It was probably done by someone she trusted.

I warned her.

My second eyelids slid into place and I saw the heat signature of one krelin that was brighter than a subtle heat that could have been mistaken for the heating vents through the walls, or even an electrical discharge from the shuttle's equipment, but the krelin has told me that he was wearing a trill robe. It helped us regulate our bodies, keeping our oils from drying out, which for other species helps dissapate their heat, but another trill knows what to look for. The heat waves from the other trill pulsed to the time of their two hearts, and the other heat signature was dull, but had the same rhythm.

I moved slowly, betting on the krelin keeping the hood of the robes low to keep my poison from finding its way to his airways. He would not spot me quickly. It was the other krelin I had to be careful of alerting him.

"There you are," he said with a chuckle. "I was hoping you would be a man of action. Our kan horns can sense our surroundings, and in this close proximity, I'm afraid for you that I'm keenly aware of any movement made in this hallway. I have no need to see you to know where you are. My warrior Li-aq is going to place this hood over your head to prevent you from poisoning us, and you are going to let him, or the owner of this robe will really have no reason to have it returned to her."

"She's alive?" I hissed, having no reason to keep silent anymore.

"For now," he said dismissively. "The queen is quite testy since her human's passing."

"The human is dead..." This would explain why they were acting now. The queen is no longer distracted with her obsession over the human mate, and now her focus has returned towards ruling Estreldez.

"We have the planet surrounded," he confirmed the situation was worse than I had predicted.

"My link satellites would have known," I objected, still clinging to hope that the protection I had been working on didn't fail us.

"Yes, that was annoying to discover," he agreed. "It's why I said surrounded, instead of being able to land. You've made invasion trickier, but not impossible. This moon is the farthest from the planet, and when timed correctly there is a gap in your net that allowed us to land here without alerting you. We will be using this shuttle to land on the planet and disable your access to activate your radiation weapon. My queen assures me that all I must do is disrupt any signals from leaving the palace, and then our ships will pass right through your net without worry of being melted. I was disappointed when she turned down my request to blow up the moon we're on now. It would have done the same job of destroying enough of the weapon you've made that using it would likely destroy more of your planet than our ships, but she insisted the planet shouldn't be harmed... for now."

"You have no idea what you are doing," I said with measured aggitation. "Belder would never trade her life for those of an entire planet."

"I thought you might say that," the large krelin adjusted their wings behind them and pulled the hood tightly about his face to protect himself. Clucking echoed through the hall, and another set of clucks responded from above me. I looked up to see a krelin drop from the ceiling. My spikes along my head hardened, and my instincts took over, spraying the room with my poison as a large blanket was smothered over me.

"You said he wouldn't spray us!" the younger krelin yelled with annoyance. I hate to disappoint, I thought with a grin. My tail swept up from under the blanket that was used to contain my poison, jabbing into the krelin that fell atop me. Our spray wasn't the only way to end a prey's life.

"Commander!" he grunted and fell to the side wheezing.

"You're not dead yet," he snapped. "Do your duty and contain the trill. Li-aq, go make sure the shuttle stays on course to launch back to planet."

"Yes, Commander."

The blanket was wrapped around my mouth, as the krelin tried to suffocate me. My teeth bared, I sunk them into his flesh. He screamed before I realized I'd been fooled as my head swayed with the whooziness of unconsciousness fast closing in. A strange smell filled my nose and burned my lungs. Their musk...

It appeared the krelins were not as dumb as I believed them to be. They may swarm and act as a collective unit, but their queen and their warriors thought enough steps ahead to wait and plan. They waited until their was an opening in the radiation net to send a single ship to land on the farthest moon Bina before anyone could detect it. They planned on disabling the entire net from within instead of directly attacking single satelites like the Almder predicted. They had an entire legion of ships waiting around the planet for the defenses to fall. And they found a way to musk this fabric, and timing the delivery of smoothering me with it before the musk could dissipate within the air.

"He'll die," the younger krelin prompted his commander.

"As will be your duty if it comes down to it," the concern easily dismissed. "It will take too much time to make sure the trill dies properly, but knowing he is out of the way and unable to contact the surface was the goal. Our warrior will be remembered as the hero that guaranteed our success. Trill poison is a death sentence, it's better to let him bleed out. Help me move the bodies off the shuttle."

"Commander," I heard the squelching noise of the other krelin gurgle out.

"You've done well," the commander said before I heard the crack of bones, and the thump of the body next to me. "Now, you're turn. I'm sure it won't kill you, but I suppose that isn't the point, is it?" He whispered next to me, "I hope you live so that you come looking for the krelin that killed your family like you did to mine. Regards from the last of Queen Sarak's hive. She was a kind queen that wanted peace until you brought the molt fever to our planet. She was my mate, and I felt the moment she died."

Then his hands wrapped around under my chin and snapped until the next thing I remember is the pain of waking from a severed spine. It wasn't the first time I'd survived such an injury. Since the injury was more from a broken nerve, it healed as soon as the nerve reconnected, but I couldn't move my head unless I could reset my spine.

"Dad?" I heard my daughter's voice.

She was alive, I thought with relief. A huge weight was lifted until I panicked that perhaps this was the afterlife. I couldn't speak yet, it hasn't been long enough to heal, or I was still on the edge of life and death.

"Mom is still unconscious," she coughed and grunted before continuing, "We are trill. You are not dead. You are not dead. Assess the situation. Your head is twisted. Reset the injury if you can, and add a medpack if hibernation isn't an option." She was keeping calm and going through the steps. This couldn't be death. I heard the crunch of bones, and pain surged through my back and head.

"Ugh, gross," she whimpered. "You better not be dead or this is the most traumatic experience I've ever had. All the comms to the main clan are broken. I don't know what to do."

Feeling returned to my jaw, and I hissed.

My Faith sucked in a sob. "You're alive."

"The link..." I choked out.

It was our last chance. With the planet surrounded, we needed to activate the radiation net, and with the comms down the only way to set off the links was to send the last satellite up with the instructions to activate upon joining the rest of the net.

"Faith! Faith!" My treasure's voice screamed in panic. "No! FAITH!" Her wails tore through my heart. She was reliving her worst nightmare of our own blessing being taken by krelins that my work failed to prevent.

"I'm here!" Faith called back. "I don't know what to do. What do we do?"

"Yueril!"

I felt the warmth of my treasure pull me close.

"He isn't breathing," Faith said with a hiccup.

"It's normal for trill bodies to hide their vitals. From heat, to breathing, and even their pulse can be so slow and nearly undetectable. Hibernation can take a long time depending on the injuries. We will keep him safe until he wakes. You're going to wake up. Do you hear me?" She rocked me in her arms, and I wished I could speak again, but I felt the way my body was fighting to stay awake. I would sleep until I was fully healed.

"He said something about the link," Faith relayed and that moment of relief that my treasure would figure it out was all it took to let go.

Hazel would do what needed to be done to save her clan. Even if it meant destroying countless krelins and burning up the deserts. There was more at stake than simple defending the planet against the krelins. They were suffering from the molt fever, and it was taking longer than we anticipated for the Ganpan Fal anti-virus to protect against the Solusgors. If the krelins are allowed to enter the planet when they are suffering great loss from the molt fever, both planets could be doomed.

Chapter
Twenty-One
Hazel

The link. He wants me to trigger the radiation net, but why? It's a last resort. There would be no need to use it unless... Unless there were ships surrounding Estreldez, but even then, Almder is adamant against the risk of high casualties on both sides.

We've discussed this. Even if the krelins invaded, we should fight in other ways first. The net was to protect against the virus.

"Faith!" I called out, not even processing that she never left my side as I stroked the scales on my mate's head. "Check the krelin they left behind."

She crinkled her nose in distaste. "Check it how? Like to see if he's still alive? He's definitely dead. Plus, I saw dad bit him. He wouldn't survive the poison."

"Look after your dad," I eased his head off my lap, and felt relief in the way his spikes along his scalp flexed as I stroked them. If he were dead, he told me that his body would grow stiff, even his scales and spikes would be unresponsive.

I moved to reach the dead krelin to confirm my suspicions. There wouldn't be much time. Pulling off the arm guards, I watched has his flesh peeled off, sticking to the leather. I struggled not to retch as I purposefully peeled more skin back to be absolutely certain. The krelin didn't move, and we could be thankful that Yueril poisoned him, otherwise this would have been a deadly encounter.

I had no choice now as I saw the purple skin underneath the torn krelin flesh. It made it here even with the Ganpan-Fal. It's too soon. We need more time. The anti-virus nano tech takes time to replicate, and we gave most of cure to Krelis. If we let it in now before the Ganpan-Fal can have more time on Estreldez... we'll all die.

Faith...

"I have to activate the link," I say quickly, finally getting up the strength to move from the shock. "Grab Loric and go to the bunker."

"But--"

"Now!"

"What about dad?"

"I've got him," I assure her as I grunt to roll him onto the thick blanket. "Why do the trill have to be so heavy. Your muscles are like rocks," I complain to stop myself from freezing in panic. I have to keep moving. "Go!"

Faith rushed off as I pulled Yueril across the floor with the blanket.

"Almder is going to murder us for this." I knew he'd say she wouldn't murder me or Faith, so I replied like he had. "You are not allowed to use that as an excuse to stay in hibernation forever. You've come back from worse. I don't want to hear that you never fully healed from your glands melting. That's just how getting old works, you know that."

It felt better to believe he could hear me, even if he couldn't. I had to believe he could so I could keep moving, keep pulling, keep trying.

Tears stung my loh as they steamed up from even a moment of thinking I'd lost him. "You are not allowed to leave me. You promised together, and if you're quitting now then that makes you a damned liar."

I knew that would make him angry. Angry was better than dead. He was a man of his word, and being called a liar was the worst insult I could say to him. Let that sink in and let that anger keep you here with me. Prove those words wrong, my rock, my love.

I made it out to the launch site, surrounded by a tarnpul pit, built to contain the explosion of sending the satellites into orbit. At the edge, I wedged Yueril into the safety zone and wraped him up in the blanket for added protection from activating the link.

Faith should be in the bunker by now, along with Loric.

I opened the control panel, and turned the crank that opened the programming slab. It would be as simple as removing the safety chip. The satellite will activate the initiation sequences as soon as it links up with the rest of the program. Without this program in place, the whole network will activate, and the only way to stop it would be to destroy this one satellite, which will happen automatically as soon as the radiation field reaches its limits and burns up the very hardware that is controlling it. Every single satellite will need to be repaired after this.

So many lives will be lost.

I whimpered.

"Who am I to play goddess, my love?"

My fingers hestitated to remove the hardware, when I saw a huge light explode from above, then a wave of wind blew through my hair, shaking my very bones as I held onto the satellite for support.

A shadow darkened the sky of the moon as too many battle ships blotted out the stars. They were destroying the net!

I pulled the hardware out and quickly cranked the heavy protective shield back in place then closed the control panel. My hand triggered the launch codes on the panel manually.

The satellite geared up and I prayed I wasn't too late. Did my hesitation mean the end of the estrelds and the krelins?

The vibration of the launch sequence under my toes as I pushed myself to run for the safety beyond the tarnpul platform.

I'm coming Yueril!

Wait for me, I pleaded as I felt the force of the launch blow me off my feet from behind. My body flew through the air, as heat burned my loh faster than it could absorb it. Fingers twitched as I reached out hoping I had made it far enough to be safe from the radiation net when it burned up the atmosphere above us.

Chapter
Twenty-Two
Li-aq

"S on, we've had to retreat," my commander's voice pierced through my mind. "You'll survive the molt fever, you have to. I know I've been tough on you, but no one can know how important you are. No one can know that you are the spawn of Queen Sarak. You are my spawn, and you will survive this. I don't have much time, they will be looking for me, but this ship will protect you as you heal."

The whirring of an engine made the images of my surroundings fuzzy. My kan ached from the interference.

"Queen Kai is protecting our species. Sending those with molt fever to die in a blaze of glory, while also securing her own clan's future. You will return to Krelis and work your way up her trusted ranks. Mate with the queen if necessary. You are the last direct spawn of Queen Sarak and you must only spawn with a queen. Do you hear me son? You will spawn a new hive and rebuild Hive Sarak. Do not fool around. There is only one krelin who knows who you are. Find her. Domsal."

When I said nothing, he repeated, "Domsal. Say the name, boy!"

I felt the sting of a hand slapping against the wound on my face from where the estreld dug out my flesh.

"Say the name!"

"Domsal," I choked out, barely aware of my surroundings.

"Good," he said again while slapping me once more to keep my conscience. "You are a prince. The only prince left of Queen Sarak. Remember who you are. Tell no one, but Domsal. She will help you."

I grunted my understanding.

My eyes opened to see my commander, and possibly my father hovering over me. His wings were charred and peeling from his bones, half his face was melted, his teeth showing through his bloody cheek, as flesh dripped from his chin.

It must have been painful to talk, I thought as he heaved above me.

"I give my life for you. Don't let it be in vain," he coughed, blood spitting on my face. "The ship still works, but the landing gears are melted, you will crash land back on Krelis. This is one of the fastest ships of the fleet. Use the grappling arms to land as safely as possible. You will orbit the planet until you wake up to land. You will wake!" He slapped me on the arm that I didn't even realize was absent from my mind. I looked down to see it was black and purple, and my father had placed a medpack directly on the injury.

"Where are you going?" I begged as he crawled on his knees and hands with his wings deformed and melted at a grotesque angle.

"They need to know I'm dead, and they need to think that the melted remains of Aram are you. No one can know you survived. Queen Sarak named you Li-aq because you were her star directly from the Goddess Lenkal. Blood of Stars."

All my life I'd thought my name meant the tears of rock, and never thought about the other definition of Li-aq.

Nectar of the Stars.

I watched as my commander fell from the ship's door, and the engines roared to life. The land was scorched outside the ship, black tarnpul sand solidified too far to see beyond. The desert turned to glassy rock, steam rising from the surface.

One truth echoed in my mind. My commander, my father, covered me with his own wings to protect me. His own body melted from the radiation, and the only medpacks on ship covered my body, not a single one was used on himself.

The door screeched into place, blinding me from the outside world. One day the trill and the estrelds would pay for their part in trying to exterminate my species.

It was the trill that sent the virus to our planet, and it was the estrelds that protected him, while their clan had the cure held protected in their labs. If I survived this molt fever then my father was right, and the estrelds held the cure all along and let our species die. Let my whole clan perish. I was all that was left.

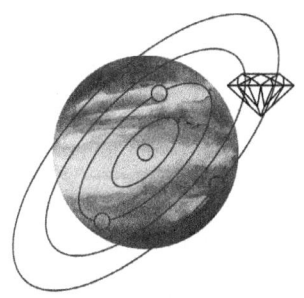

Chapter
Twenty-Three
Hazel

Two rotations of the largest moon signaled another mating cycle was approaching, and as defeated as my clan felt, there was hope in the air. The krelins were shown the might of the radiation net, and with the destruction of many of their fleets they retreated. They were safer to return to their planet where the nano technology could replicate more within them to save them from the molt fever that they've come to call the Solusgors virus.

And with more time, Estreldez could replicate the Gan-pan-Fal and protect ourselves from future outbreaks. It was difficult for estrelds with the radiation making the replication process slower, but it was working. Blood tests showed an increase of the anti-viral technology adapting to the radiation, and surviving.

And my sister was finally growing, though much more slowly than we'd ever seen a birth progress before. Luan was so small, and in no hurry to leave her egg. Almder feared that she would be a still birth and join the rest of our siblings with the goddess, returning the rock. Ezra has been monitoring Luan's progress closely but has seen enough growth to be hopeful.

Much of the clan visits the Almder to add their own radiation to her belly for nourishment and look upon the princess as a sign of the clan's prosperity.

As long as Luan lives, so too does the clan.

"You know you're a princess too," Faith says with a pout.

"You'll always be my princess, and that should be enough for both of us," I reply. "Unless you'd like us to announce to the krelins that you are the Almder's granddaughter and are somehow compatible with mating a krelin? I'm sure you won't be abducted and find a new krelin mate as soon as they recover."

"Mom!" she groaned. "That's really twisted. You know he died melted in the dark land desert."

"Is that what it's being called now?" I cringed.

"I wouldn't worry on it," Yueril said while wrapping his tail around my leg. The heat of his tincture oil made my thighs clench together. I glared at him playfully to tell him now was not the time with our daughter in the room. "With your mate dead, you'll be able to be more careful about who you choose to bite, but Loric brought up a good point that your ability to withstand the musk is a valuable asset to protecting the clan. I'm also working on a breathing apparatus that can be inserted into the nose and neutralize the musk."

"We can talk about this after the mating ceremony. You've been looking forward to watching one, haven't you? I remember my own mother tried to stop me from going, and it only made me want to see it more. You may watch, but you will stay with Loric and no using your oil to go wandering or I'll have to make sure you stay on Bina the next time there's a ceremony."

"I'll behave," she promised, though I could see the mischief in her eyes.

"See that you do," I said with a stern stare.

"I swear!"

"Losing a mate, even an unintentional one, is rough," Yuriel assured me and then sighed. "It's likely you'll struggle to find another mate for a while, at least until you decide to have Ezra remove that mark on your neck."

Faith lifted her hand to her shoulder unconsciously to feel that the mark was still there. The trill heal better than most species, and since the mark never went away, it only confirmed that they bonded. It was best that he was gone. It was much too soon for me to accept my offspring was growing up. At her age I was still living in the mountain and my mother was still alive.

Though the Almder was who spawned me, my mother gave up everything to protect me, even her life.

I smiled to myself, knowing how true that was for me now. I'd do the same for Faith.

She ran off to the shuttle with Loric, leaving Yueril and me to keep watch from the farthest moon Bina. Estreldez below us was forever changed because of us. A dark side of the planet where the moon's rays do not reach. The tarnpul there is dangerous and very little radiation lives where the land was sucked dry.

The radiation net worked, but at great cost.

"We destroyed this world..." I said with a shiver.

"We gave it more time," he objected. "And many estrelds were able to survive the drain on the planet."

"We don't know how many were lost to the dark land."

"But we do know how many are still alive." He kissed my temple and whispered in my ear, "Let me hold the guilt that grows within you. Let me ease that burden. I brought the world destroyer to Krelis instead of to Estreldez. I made that choice to build up the immunity to the Solusgors with what we had left lingering in our ship. It left Estreldez vulnerable as we waited for Krelis to adapt. There was no way to know that the radiation here would slow our progress. Place blame where it is deserved, on the Solusgors Virus."

He's right, I tried to convince myself. But I needed help, and we couldn't combat the virus on our own. I had to find a way to bring more researchers to face the problem. This wasn't the end to the fight of our lives.

To our offspring's lives.

I'd almost lost everything.

His tail went down below my knee and I lost the feel of him, but imagined the tingle that could have been. Reminded of the time he gently tended to my feet when we first met. Then his tail rubbed its oils up my thigh and I gasped at the way my skin responded, my mating loh vibrating for touch. He was always touching me to make sure I never felt the pain for long. His touch wasn't meant to be demanding, just a lovely caress to keep the pain at bay, but after all these risings I needed more.

"You glow brighter than any treasure I've had the pleasure to witness," he whispered at my lobe, his tongue flicking out to steam at the loh below my ear.

I moaned as his fingers kneaded into my lower back, his oils coating the burns there. The motor chair was temporary until Ezra could finish her prosthetics for my legs. She'd make them out of the finest and sturdiest rock and promised they would function as well as any other. I knew there would be no more running, but I guess that was the point of staying on Estreldez this whole time. Running away was never the intent.

Lifting my chin up, I laced my fingers behind his neck to pull him down to my lips. He moaned into my mouth, and I knew we had both missed this.

My skin tingled as I tugged his hand from my back and moved it around my hips to sink between my thighs.

"Are you sure?" he mumbled into our kiss, but that didn't stop his fingers from slipping into my heat.

It was mating season, and the moon's rays were at their peak. Bina may have been the farthest moon from Estreldez, but it still pulled radiation from the stardust swirling within the galaxy.

My hips bucked up, making my butt slide down the chair, stopped only by his tail wrapped around my thigh.

He groaned. "Where do you think you're going, Treasure?"

I giggled like I had a choice in sliding off the chair, but I liked the way he still made me feel whole. My hand clung to behind his head while the other gripped his forearm, as his fingers rubbed at my entrance. My breath hitched as I felt myself open for him.

He teased a finger inside before I gripped his wrist and shook my head, biting his lip. Yueril hissed, but paused for direction.

"I want to remember like it's the first time," I panted.

Knowing what I was asking for, his tail flicked up my leg, and waited near where I grabbed his wrist. I used his neck as support to adjust myself, and grabbed hold of his tail. He braced himself on the armrests of my chair, allowing me to use his support to guide myself atop his tip. My lip trembled as his tail entered me, and I paused to feel the fullness of the moment. My mate always wished to see me shine. I saw that now as I did in the past. I was never lacking in his eyes.

Even now.

"You are brighter than any sun," he whispered to me as I moved against him.

My hips trembled and yet he waited, allowing me to do this for myself. My arms were growing weary from holding myself up by his neck, and he simply moved his arms underneath mine until I shuddered, clamping down on his tail.

"Your turn is over, My Treasure." He lifted me from the chair and took me to our bed. His tongue lapped up the juices dripping down my legs then slithered across my clit. I gasped as he licked and suckled like I held his life inside of me.

"I've wanted nothing more than to have all of you inside me since the moment I knew we both lived yet again. Your essence on my tail, on my tongue, and soon on my cock. I must bathe in your pleasure or I fear I will not survive another rising."

I smiled and laughed for the first time since the Great Surge, as the net failure was now called. "That is not part of a trill anatomy to die from not tasting their mate."

His eyes hooded with lust as he replied between my legs, "It is very much a cause of great many trill deaths to be dehydrated, and I have been without this life-giving nectar for too long."

His tongue lapped at my mating loh and I moaned with a shiver before the cool air of his absence made me reopen my eyes with disappointment.

He smiled down at me with a wicked grin, knowing exactly what he was doing to me. His tail rubbed at my cheek where I could smell my own pleasure on his scales. "Not a drop will be wasted. I will taste you even as I fill you with my seed."

"Your seed is mine," I teased him as I brought his tail to my lips and licked my own juices from its tip.

He growled and gripped my hips roughly to position his cock at my entrance, but stopped just before filling me, making me whimper.

I felt the way his scales flexed along his shaft, teasing my thighs. After many cycles, I found a few spots of my own to tease. My fingers prodded at his tail tip until the spike within eased out. He knew now that as dangerous as he was, he wouldn't harm me. He shivered as I licked along the tender flesh that connected his spike to the inside of his nerves within his tail. Finding these little spots of vulnerability made me ache even more for him that he let me know every part of him.

He pressed his cock within my mating loh slowly stretching me as he let me rub gently at his tail's nerves. He licked his lips and rubbed the sore loh at my hips, his oils soothing me and building a fire in my belly.

"Every part of me is yours," he grunts as he sinks deeper inside. My loh burn, glowing brightly, warming from the inside out, and as his cock swells and his scales flutter against my walls I feel everything. I feel the way my toes would curl as my heels dug into his ass to push him farther. The ache in my muscles as I begged for him to reach that spot so deep it makes me forget there was ever such a thing as being apart from him.

I squeezed my eyes shut, wanting to live in that moment of blissful fullness for as long as possible. His tail tapped at my chin and with the spike retracted he swiped up the tears with his smooth scales. I shook my head, refusing to open my eyes and know that my legs were missing beyond my knees.

His claws squeezed my hips and I squeaked with a pout before I gasped at his cock hitting a throbbing bundle of nerves sending pleasure back to my phantom toes.

"Treasure," he insisted with a hiss.

I couldn't deny him. I opened my eyes to see the affection from his yellow eyes strike me to my core. "Look how beautiful you are. Look how you affect me. Feel how you make me burn," he said with an adoration of a devoted worshipper of the goddess herself. Under his gaze I felt like I could build worlds, breathe life into stars and span the universe with a single explosive leap.

Moving in and out, he thrust with powerful purpose like each movement was trying to fill me with his feelings. How much he needed me, how much he wanted me to know what I meant to him was being pumped inside of me. His cock quivered against my nerves, expanding and warming with the friction. His touch cooled the heat of my loh and made be glow with warmth all at once. I moaned as he grunted with each forceful slap of his hips against mine. His cock pulsed against the pleasurable spot that yearned for more pressure.

Faster, and harder until our lungs panted for air only the other could provide. He leaned down to give me the very breath he needed to live as our lips met with a hunger that had nothing to do with our gut, but everything to do with our hearts.

I could feel him now, like this. The thumping of his heart pumping from the blood working to join us as one, engorging his cock to fill me with his pleasure that only I can give him.

"Take me, Treasure. That's it!" he grunted as I clamped around him, squeezing him from the inside to lock us together in ecstasy.

"Every last drop," he promised with gentle kisses along my jaw, "Every part of me is yours."

I reveled in the way his cock throbbed and the heated ache of release thundered through every nerve in my body, making me glow.

My loh felt renewed and the pain of loss was gone. I knew my legs were gone, and no matter what contraption Ezra was able to make for me, that wouldn't change. But I never felt more whole.

Almost losing everything that was important to me reminded me what I was fighting for.

It wasn't just my future.

We were fighting for this feeling for generations to come. One day, even my Faith would get to have this completeness of finding her purpose. With or without a mate, but mine certainly made it easier to be reminded I'm not broken, no matter what came my way to break me down.

"You make me whole," I panted into his ear.

"No, Treasure. I'm just a needy trill that wants to feel the sun on my scales. You burn brightly without me, I simply beg to see it burn more often or I will not survive another rising."

I chuckled, swatting at him playfully. "Are you blackmailing the sun?"

"If that is what it takes to feel your warmth, I will gladly be your villain."

Nuzzling his nose, I then pulled him into my arms. "You aren't the villain. I stole something much more precious than a star. A star has no choice on if it explodes, it relies on outside forces to determine if it should destroy or create new stars. So, I pulled you into my orbit and we created a new star to help protect this universe."

But our star won't be alone.

I've been working on putting a message into the nano tech, searching the universe for beings capable of defending against the Solusgors when we are gone.

It's up to the next generation, I thought with pride.

Come and find me.

We are the breaker of stars, and together we will explode. It's up to us to make the time we borrowed enough to stop the stars from ending.

"What are you thinking, Treasure?"

I shook my head and pulled him tighter.

"Small stars fade, my heart. But if all the stars join together, they will make one magnificent nebula, not even the Solusgors would defeat such an event."

"From your lips to the universe."

The Beginning...

Continue the Treasures of Trillume Series with book one, Jewel of the Alien Bandit with Luan. Or book two, Her Alien Prince with Prince Trent from Krelis. Both are standalone with parallel timelines, read in any order. And continue learning more about the Trillume Universe with each standalone romance as they layer the more your read!

https://books.steviemarie.com/TreasuresofTrillume

* * *

Newsletter

Join Sky Robert's Weekly Newsletter. Read Her Alien Exchnge for free: https://books.steviemarie.com/heralienexchange

Author Note

T hank you for reading Her Alien Starbreaker! Help support indie by rating and leaving a review! I am 100% human, and if you ever find any typos, I'm happy to fix them so the next reader has an even better experience just email me: skyrobertromances(at)gmail(dot)com. Be sure to include the subject: TypoKiller and the name of the book.

This is an origin story of the Trillume Universe and how the Ganpan-Fal, World Destroyer virus, (Or anti-virus depending on how you think about it) made its way to the outreaches of the galaxy to the planet Sholunus, Krelis, Necias Delta Fal, and Estreldez. The Trillume Universe is filled with standalone romances within an interwoven plot across all books. I created this particular story because throughout the series the trill are pretty much the boogie aliens of the universe, the unknown evil that started everyone else's problems, but I thrive on stories that bridge the grey area and the multiple facets of life where someone's evil is the hero of their own story. Thus, this story was brought to life.

I know you may be left with questions about what happens to the Birds or Zorn, Vareo, Genbi, and the human left with the krelins, and there are answers to all of those questions... eventually, as the universe unravels one book at a time. Every book in the Trillume Universe is a standalone romance but has an evolving interwoven plot overarching every book. The more books you read the more you'll learn about the universe and different characters in it. You can read more about Vareo, as well as return to Estreldez, with Jewel of the Alien Bandit

And yes, the book is also a standalone, but know that Luan and Vareo's story isn't finished, there is more to tell for them and out of all the couples in the Trillume Universe they will be given a book two! Find out more about the krelins and what happens with their planet in Her Alien Prince and Her Alien Insurgent. Want to know what happened to the necia warriors spoken about as being conquered by the queen of the trill? Check out Her Alien Savior, Her Alien Warrior, and soon to come Her Alien Captor! You can start reading Her Alien Exchange for free today by joining my newsletter: https://books.steviemarie.com/heralienexchange

If you are wondering if Faith will be given her own story, YES! Li-aq, Gho-ran, and Faith will return in Book Four, the book after Her Alien Insurgent with a bit of an enemy to lovers trope. Their book does not have a title yet. I plan on finishing up Her Alien Captor and Her Alien Delegate first, as there hasn't been enough read through on Her Alien Insurgent for me to write the continuation with their story. You get a brief mention of Faith in Her Alien Insurgent as she gets abducted by a certain krelin, but that's another story, isn't it?

Help support the Trillume Universe by sending the love with sharing your thoughts by review/rating on the anthology, but also on the book itself on Goodreads here: https://www.goodreads.com/book/show/220073374-h er-alien-starbreakerThis story launched separately in an anthology Beyond Earth with sixteen chapters. This newly launched edition has twenty-three chapters, nearly fifteen thousand extra words with a new beginning chapter and an extended ending. It also has the beautifully commissioned artwork by Deborah Garcia. Don't forget to share your love of the Trillume Universe to other alien lovers and let me know what you think of Her Alien Starbreaker!

Are you excited to read what's next in the universe? Are there other characters you want to see more of? Your excitement and suggestions help fuel ideas and nudge me towards writing the next book as fast as my fingers can rub some words onto a page, so keep cheering!

Follow along on what's coming, see teasers, progress, what I'm reading, exclusive goodies, or just say, "hi", join my newsletter and grab Her Alien Exchange for freesies, or join the Sky's Smut Between the Pages on Facebook! I hang out on Instagram more often than Twitter these days, so give me a follow: @authorsteviemarie

Thank you so much for being a fan of my alien romances, it means the world to my squishy heart.

Sky

xoxo

About the Author

SKY ROBERT

Sky Robert is a mom of two tiny humans in training, narrates audiobooks for fantasy/sci-fi indie authors, and when she isn't writing (which is MOST of the time) you can find her consuming copious amounts of coffee, promoting indie authors, reading alien smut, fantasy, sci-fi and romance books, chowing down on Indian butter chicken, and when she actually hangs out with people in person, in real life, outside of the internet, (gasps) she's playing board or card games. All around nerd, lover of the strange, and all things fantastical.

Grab your first free alien monster fated mates romance Her

Alien Exchange for free when you join the Romance Newsletter: https://sendfox.com/lp/m2gyw5

Books By Sky:

Treasures of Trillume:

Jewel of the Alien Bandit https://book.steviemarie.com/jotab

Her Alien Prince https://book.steviemarie.com/heralienprince

Her Alien Insurgent! https://books.steviemarie.com/heralieninsurgent

Her Alien Savior https://book.steviemarie.com/heraliensavior

Her Alien Warrior: https://books.steviemarie.com/heralienwarrior

Her Alien Exchange https://book.steviemarie.com/heralienexchange

Books by S.M. McCoy:

Taking Medusa: Romantasy Greek Myth Retelling https://book.steviemarie.com/takingmedusa

GRUMPY WARRIORS THAT WORSHIP THEIR MATES

NECIA WARRIORS

An Alien Space Vampires Fated Mates Romance series, each a standalone adventure filled with spice and plot, world building, exhibitionism, powerful love, and troubled heroes with flaws to fall for. Knotting peens that bond their mates, giving them prolonged health to match their lifespan.

Take a look at book one here...

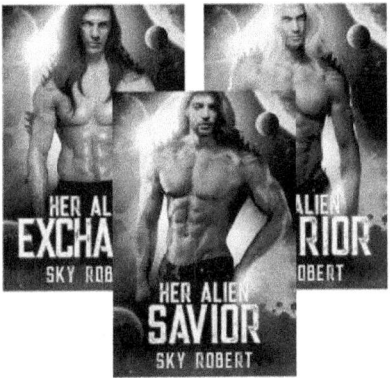

Necia Alien Warriors

Violet

Human Exchange Trade, H.E.T., was my ticket off Earth. Leaving the planet to get away was probably an over correction and impulsive, but I needed a change. And what bigger change was there than to hop on a shuttle to a large spaceship that would take me to an alien host on the planet ASunGor for a year. I get to learn a new culture, fool around with a few hot aliens, and come back to Earth with a better perspective on my life. At least, that's what I thought, before I rushed the whole thing, and my host wasn't there to pick me up. Another exchange girl named Evie was heading to the planet Necias Prime looking terrified, and I had time to kill, so what harm was there in taking a detour to make sure she was okay? I mean, my reasons had nothing to do with the sexy alien that had come to escort her.

Commander Roe-el

I was reluctant to leave Princess Klemon's protection when she told me to escort a human to my home planet for a mating experiment, but in my haste to return to her side, I left without asking the name of the human. When I got to the station... there were two of them waiting, and one of them was making me regret not having tasted a female in years. Her scent did things to me, and I found myself going into rut when it was my job as commander to protect the humans, not screw them. Humans were much too fragile for a necia warrior, but the fire in her eyes made me question my priorities, and I couldn't say no when she boarded my ship. Everything inside of me needed to claim her, but she needed to say, yes, first.

Dive into a fated mates, spicy monster love romance with instalust, exhibitionism, strong female empowerment, alpha male with consent, and alien extremities. Join the fated mates of the alien warriors of Necias Prime in the Treasures of Trillume Universe. All stand-alone romances, within a fun interwoven plot of the universe.

VIOLET

As soon as the Human Exchange Training was open to the public, I was first in line to join. That might seem reckless, to immediately seek to abandon Earth for a year-long, alien-job training program, but anything was better than what I had going for me now. My ex was psychotic, and he didn't take my whole let's-be-friends conversation as well as I'd hoped. You really don't see all the red flags until the end. Sure, I was feeling uncomfortable with him for a few months now, but all that crazy made for great sex and had my mind all addled over the idea of leaving him simply because he seemed a bit clingy when I wanted to hang out with the girls. I had a decent job as a marketing consultant for what used to be the biggest IT company. But ever since we—meaning humans—were introduced to how big the galaxy was by these aliens called the Trill, well, our IT was way behind the times.

Too many people were more obsessed with the technology the aliens had to offer instead of what mere human mortals were working on. IT took a huge dive, and so did my career. I was a bartender now; that's how I met Mick... and he needed some time to cool off and find a new obsession. Living for a year with aliens while also getting training in a new career sounded like a win-win.

I left the recruitment center more excited than ever after being accepted by an alien host from some planet called ASunGor. It wasn't too far from the planet Trillume, which was where the trill were from. ASunGor was beautiful, with its purples, yellows, and oranges, and red gaseous clouds that, if they didn't tell me otherwise, I might have thought were poisonous. Red was usually associated with warnings, like my ex with all of his red flags. But I was assured the red was merely a reaction to the iron particles in the air hitting the oxygen, and the concentration was mostly in the atmosphere, not on the surface where there was a reasonable amount of breathable air for humans to survive without any harm.

I got a data packet about the aliens that lived there sent to my brain implant, which was updated with an alien language translator, so all that was left was to wait for the transport shuttle to take me to the ship waiting in Earth's orbit. I'd be gone for a year.

Before I could think on it more, I was interrupted by a cringe-worthy voice that was all too sickeningly familiar. Damn it. I had been so careful about getting here without being followed.

"What do you think you're doing, Violet?" he said from behind me, leaning against the brick wall of the recruitment center.

Clearing my throat, I jutted a hip out in defiance while replying, "None of your business, Mick."

He rubbed his gorgeous face with his hands in exasperation. That's what got me the first time around. Mick was too damned pretty, and I let that cloud my judgement for too long. The kind of sweet, chiseled pretty that made you think he was both adoring and capable of sinful things. And he certainly was capable of all sorts of sinful things that I used to look forward to—with relish—but it wasn't worth it.

"I know the IT industry has seen a dive, and you weren't looking to be a bartender your whole life, but offworlding? Come on, Violet, that's low; even for you. There have been plenty of news stories about how most of those aliens want to experiment with us, and a pretty girl like you... Violet, if you need a good fuck, you don't need to jump on a shuttle to find it," Mick said with equal parts disgust and interest. It was amazing how he could twist his words to both insult me and imply that his dick was good enough for the job, all at the same time.

I smiled sweetly at him, but anyone with eyes could see my derision as I retorted, "Oh, honey. I don't have to go anywhere for a good fuck. I've got myself covered just fine." I showed him my two favorite fingers and then lowered one to leave only the middle, silently saying 'Go fuck yourself' and ending with a little wink. It wasn't right to tease him. He liked it when I played hard to get, but I wasn't playing at anything this time. I was more than happy with my own company. Anything was better than the constant, back-handed compliments I received from him regularly. At least my own fingers knew my clit was bigger than just the tip that was visible. It was a whole fucking organ, and he wasn't its musician anymore.

Mick pushed off from the wall, and my whole body froze like a deer caught in headlights. I talked a big game, but the dark look in his eyes was terrifying and crazed. That same determined gaze used to make me smile, knowing we were about to have some great hate sex. But when I wanted it to end, the feelings changed, and he wasn't willing to let me go. I gulped back my fear as he slowly approached, but my feet wouldn't budge. His knuckles brushed against my cheek, and I instinctively pulled my face away before he harshly pinched my chin in his grasp to force me to look at him.

"You know you like it when that foul mouth of yours wraps around my cock before you scream my name. Your fingers can still do whatever they want when I'm fucking the sin from your dirty thoughts," he purred, pushing his mouth on to mine. My hands scrambled to find purchase, to shove him off, but he held me firm, and I struggled to slide my mouth away from his, gasping for air.

"Get off of me," I growled, and he released me at the same time as I shoved, making me stumble backwards and I lost my balance. He let me trip, falling to my ass, and he shook his head at me like I was a piece of trash that he'd have to pick up for the betterment of the world. I wiped his saliva from my cheek and forced myself to spit at his feet, to rid the taste of him from my tongue. "You're disgusting."

It wasn't that I didn't particularly like dirty talk; I did. But the way he said things was anything but endearing. It was possessive in a way that made my skin crawl. Like I needed to burn the clothes I was wearing to get the feeling of his hands groping me seared from my memory.

"No one will touch you the way you want it like I do, Violet. Not even an alien dick, if they even have one, would touch you after they found out what makes you scream," he threatened while licking his lips, trying to get me to think about all the things he wanted to do with his tongue. "Don't make me wait too long; this game of yours is getting old." Mick left me there sitting in what I now realized was a puddle left by the rain from the night before. It certainly wasn't my own juices that had soaked through my pants this time.

"Fucker," I gritted out, getting back to my feet and stomping back to the recruitment center. I opened the door a little more aggressively than I'd intended, but I was amped and pissed. Waiting for the later shuttle to "gather" my shit wasn't an option anymore. I was leaving tonight, even if I had to sign some extra waivers or agree to an extended exchange program. I didn't give a crap. I was leaving now!

Mick was lucky I ever touched his dick, and he was right. The game was getting old, but not the one he thought we were playing. I was sick and tired of him harassing me, and the authorities said there wasn't enough to get a restraining order. Not that it would have stopped him, I thought with disdain.

"Miss Thorn... did you forget something?" my recruiter, Beth, asked with a quirked brow at my now soaked pants and probably reddened face.

"Yes, I need you to get me on the next shuttle."

Beth pursed her lips as if I were insane. "You have no personal items with you. And usually people wish to say goodbye to their friends, family, someone before they go. You should really wait for the next shuttle in a few weeks," she insisted.

"No," I snapped before calming myself to reiterate in a less intimidating tone. "I want to leave on the one I overheard you saying was leaving today." I paused, then added, "Please." I forced a smile to my face and waited for her to deny me because what I was asking for was ridiculous. It was the most insane thing I'd ever asked of someone.

She lowered her voice and wrapped her arm around my shoulder to lead me away from the prying eyes of the other recruits in the lobby, eying me with concern. "Are you in trouble?"

I sighed, not wanting to get into this with practically a stranger, but she seemed so sweet and trustworthy, unlike my usual friends I hung out with. They were more encouraging of my bad choices. This was not a bad choice though, I reassured myself. This was crazy, but it wasn't a bad choice. As far as decisions went, sure, I should probably wait for my scheduled shuttle in a few weeks. But what did I have to lose besides a creepy ex and girlfriends that didn't even know a single thing about me, other than I was fun to have a drink with? Come to think of it, they probably mostly liked the cheap drinks I got for working at the bar... I shook my head. I was over the whole thing.

"I've got an ex stalking me, and a year away will be good for both of us," I admitted, but I didn't let her know that a sick part of me knew that if I didn't get on this shuttle, two weeks was a long time, and I didn't think I had the strength to resist Mick when he reflected on his actions in a day or two. He'd come back, sweeter than ever, and we'd have mind-blowing hate sex, and I'd hate myself even more for letting him get under my skin. I deserved better than what he was offering. I knew that in theory. But in practice... he was right. I was fucked up, and I liked how he made me feel when he wasn't being a petty asshole. He knew how I liked to be touched.

This was for me. I needed to recalibrate my brain and my body.

I didn't need his kind of possessive veneration.

"Yes, but you won't have time to go home and grab personal items. No matter how strong a person is, everyone gets Earth sick and misses the smallest of things that remind them of Earth when they are away." Beth was trying to talk me out of it, and she was doing a shitty job. I didn't give a crap if I missed the dirt or way pizza tasted. Sometimes, cold turkey was the best way to change your bad habits. I'd just keep myself busy to distract myself.

"Beth, I see what you're doing here, and it's sweet, really. But if you don't let me on that shuttle, my life is more screwed than if you let me leave. Trust me." I could see her lips press into a fine line as she led me through the building, probably to a holding cell because I was likely to harm one of us if they didn't board me on the shuttle today. I was that kind of desperate, and pretty much too angry to see reason beyond what I'd set my mind to.

She sighed in what I hoped was resignation, but it easily could have been her annoyance at another crazy she had to deal with in a diplomatic way.

"Violet." She used my first name, which was weird. "You have to be sure about this. The shuttle is boarding now. Once you're on, there is no coming back until your exchange is completed. Do you understand?"

Well, that was unexpected.

"Like, now, now?" My nerves were getting the better of me, and I was just as likely to bolt as I was to follow through with my hare-brained idea of jumping on a shuttle to a different planet.

She laughed, which was refreshing to hear, before she nodded her agreement.

This was happening.

I was leaving.

She was going to let me on the shuttle.

ROE-EL

The Princess of Trillume rolled her eyes at me, and I grumbled. Princess or not, she was asking me to do something that was akin to fucking an animal.

"My Princess, I think I misheard you. I apologize." I tried to show my disinterest without actually outright denying her orders of me. I was a reputable warrior, and I'd never questioned my position to be in her service, but this was too much. She must understand that if any other had asked this of me, I would have considered it an insult that would have been remedied by a duel before I agreed to anything more. Only if I failed would I submit myself to this. My upper lip snarled.

"You didn't mishear," she confirmed with a sly smile. "I need you to train a human in the ways of the Necia and encourage this human to attempt spawning with a Necia warrior. It's important to my research. I'm not asking you to be the warrior that attempts procreation with the human, Commander Roe-el. I'm asking you to escort the human to Necias Prime and train them before they arrive, while encouraging the human to be open-minded about your species."

"You're asking me to have another warrior," I paused to wrinkle my nose at the prospect, "spawn with a human. Do you have any idea what you're asking of any Necia you have do that? Humans are fragile, and deserving of our protection, but they are like pets to us that we've used as entertainment and companionship on long missions across the galaxies. They are NOT mates," I insisted with disgust.

Princess Klemon nodded. "I'm aware. They are not so barbaric to be considered animals, Commander Roe-el. They are just... different, and, according to my research, potentially compatible mates as well. You are assigned to go pick them up right about... well, now. You should head out if you are to get there on time. I know how you like to be punctual."

"Princess, my assignment is to you. Not your project. I would be derelict in my duties to leave—"

"Commander," she stopped me before I could finish. "The project is the reason why you are needed to protect me at all. If it makes you feel any better, I'll be sure to stay hidden in the lab until your return. You're the only one I trust to escort our exchange human to their new host. You won't be gone longer than a few weeks. There and back."

I narrowed my eyes, uncertain if I could trust her to stay within the lab walls while I was away and still grossed out by the idea of mating with a human.

With a huff, she added, "I'll stay put."

"I will not mate with a human," I clarified.

She shook her head in a manner that made me think she thought I was humorous, which made my shoulder epaulets twitch in agitation.

"I'm not asking you to be the one to mate with the human. I already have a willing warrior who is trustworthy and understands my research and what it means to the whole galaxy, not just Necias Prime," Princess Klemon explained, then did that hand motion she used to shoo me away from her research.

"Fine, but if I find that you have left this lab for whatever reason, you will be hard-pressed to have me leave your side in the future. Keep that in mind, should you get the desire to go exploring without protection." It was my job to make sure her family didn't find her and that anyone who knew what she was working on didn't find her. She was right; her research was too important to risk. If she thought I was needed to protect the human, then that is what I would do for her.

Arriving at the waystation, I grumbled, realizing Klemon had tricked me into thinking I was going to be late when I was actually early. Wasting my time waiting grated on my nerves like no other feeling. She was being cheeky when she said I preferred to be punctual, I knew that. I always arrived on time... never early. If I'm to be somewhere at a time, that is the time I arrive. No earlier, no later. On time.

And here I was, waiting like a fool for some human to disembark from their transport to Trillume and then reboard my shuttle to head out to Necias Prime. All the human exchanges came to Trillume first, then to their destinations. Never a direct route, as the humans were strictly monitored and accounted for. Couldn't have secret humans being stowed away and sold off in the markets. We'd never hear the end of it. There would be an open war between species about who had more rights to the humans and to Earth. The only good thing about that was I wouldn't be bored on my glorified babysitter duties of a princess. I might get a few duels in here and there.

The humans left the shuttle and appeared as I expected them to be: like scared animals, shifting uncomfortably around until a new owner came to take them to their temporary homes. One by one, they were being plucked away by ambassadors from various planets claiming their right to have their own human for a while. I realized I hadn't asked which one I should be acquiring for her highness' research. I mean, there wasn't much difference between them all, was there? Did it matter which one I brought with me?

I liked the look of the larger human that appeared to be less likely to be harmed by our Necia females. He would stand a chance of surviving Necias Prime with his muscles, though he still wasn't quite as bulky as I would have preferred to ensure his safety. I cursed under my breath, remembering that Klemon had said there was a warrior who'd agreed to mate with a human, and I hadn't asked if they were female or male. I waited a bit longer to see if another planet was claiming the human male. Shortly, I found out that someone had indeed chosen this male for their own exchange.

There were only two females left after the rush, and I found myself unable to remove my eyes from the one with bright red hair, the color of Necias's oceans. Unlike the other female, who appeared as frightened as I would expect of most who ventured so far from their habitats, this one folded her arms over her chest, highlighting small mounds that had my mouth quirking up in interest. I closed my eyes to rid myself of the thought.

Did humans possess some kind of lure not recorded in their data assessments? Not one warrior had ever spoke of this kind of attraction at the mere sight of the curves of a human's frame. Possibly it was my subconscious playing tricks on me after the discussion I'd had with Klemon. She had planted this idea of fucking with humans, and I had been without a female for some time because of my current assignment. It was difficult to acquire interest, or even spur on a rut, with a protective detail and not many options for duels. There had been no need to prove my strength and encourage my use of bed play.

But there that human was, and, when I opened my eyes, I was still enthralled by her curves and the strong stance of what I could only imagine was her annoyance at waiting there for her host. I blinked, regaining my composure. Waiting for me, I thought, and a sudden surge rippled through my body, sending a jolt to my cock. What on Horv's great vine was happening to me? This couldn't possibly be a rut, could it? Was I so far gone that merely the idea of mating and the mission back to Necias Prime had sent my body into rut? Had I waited so long in a boring assignment that my body found any excuse to claim and conquer even an animal such as this human?

I grimaced, but that didn't stop my eyes from watching as the female adjusted her hips to favor her other leg. Those silvery eyes of hers looked out in search of her alien host, and it was only her and the other female left. What kind of ambassador arrived late to pick up their human? Sure, I was making mine wait, but I was here. Surely the other host would know who they were supposed to pick up.

Wasting time was making my mind wander, and thinking of that human's small, fleshy mounds pressed against me instead of those small arms wasn't doing me any favors in improving my mood. I refused to rut with a human, it was an abuse of my strength to claim such a weak being in such a manner. Humans were helpless creatures that needed protecting, not warriors—or even broodmares—capable of taming a Necia warrior's epulknot in rut. I'm not a monster, I repeated to myself in an attempt to calm the hardening length down my thigh. I had to pick up Klemon's human before I decided to call this whole thing off. I'd just grab the human that didn't make me doubt my sanity and be done with it.

Approaching the females, I tried to move slowly as to not frighten them further, and the dark-haired female flinched and tugged at the other's arm in warning. It was wise for humans to fear a Necia warrior. This female had good instincts for self-preservation. We were predators in this ecosystem. And yet, years of evolution did not stop the other from lifting a brow and smirking at me in challenge.

"It's about time. I was wondering if I had to walk over and get you. Didn't anyone ever teach you that it's rude to keep a lady waiting?" she snapped off in succession. Her words stunned me momentarily as my translator had to catch up with the harsh, yet intriguing, sound of her voice. I towered over her stature and yet there she was, chin held firm as she stared me down. Those silvery eyes had flecks of gold, now that I was close enough to see it, and I could see her beneath me as I tried to count every star in her mesmerizing portals and plunged into her depths. My mouth salivated, and my cock pulsed, seeking a reprieve I could not grant it. This was too far, even for a rut-inflicted mind. I had to control myself.

She was a human.

Not some seductive warrior seeking sport on my epulknot.

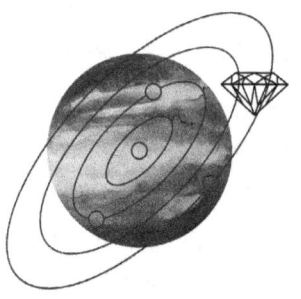

Her Alien Exchange

Read this book for free and join my author newsletter:
https://dl.bookfunnel.com/f2fwrjww4p

She thought joining the alien exchange would only
be for a year...

Want More?

For more information about upcoming books in the Treasures of Trillume or Necia Warrior Series (or any other books by Sky Robert) like me on Facebook or subscribe to my newsletter.

Check out more books by Sky Robert and follow on Bookbub: https://www.bookbub.com/authors/sky-robert

Thanks for reading! You are a book hero!

xoxo, all the squishies,

Sky

https://linktr.ee/skyrobertromances

www.ingramcontent.com/pod-product-compliance
Lightning Source LLC
Chambersburg PA
CBHW060548260626
47161CB00003B/1110